THUNDER TRAIL

The prairie surrounding Redmon, Texas is a cattlemen's empire, where the barons of the open range live in almo feudal splendour. But the railroad is fighting its w to the territory, attended by tumult, violence and . There are plenty of people whose fervent wish halt its disruptive progress — including a vicio asked outlaw who strikes mercilessly in the darl cking trains, robbing and killing. Walt Slade, stal indercover agent of the Texas Rangers and fast unslinger in the Southwest, is given the job of h ug him down, but his reputation precedes him: rely has he set foot in the town when three gunm try to put him in an early grave. Can Slade eluc llets and dynamite long enough to force a she vn with the head of the gang, and restore pea the land?

THUNDER TRAIL

BRADFORD SCOTT

SAGEBRUSH
Large Print Westerns

First published in the United States by Pyramid Books

First Isis Edition
published 2019
by arrangement with
Golden West Literary Agency

A catalogue record for this book is available
from the British Library.

ISBN 978–1–78541–684–2 (pb)

Published by
F. A. Thorpe (Publishing)
Anstey, Leicestershire

Set by Words & Graphics Ltd.
Anstey, Leicestershire
Printed and bound in Great Britain by
T. J. International Ltd., Padstow, Cornwall

This book is printed on acid-free paper

CHAPTER
ONE

The Comanche Indians were credited with naming it, but the Thunder Trail was old long before the Comanche appeared in Texas.

Doubtless in the beginning it was a buffalo track, beaten out by the hoofs of the great beasts in the course of their seemingly senseless migrations. The splayfeet of prehistoric men padded it. Legend says that the clanking armor of Coronado's iron men of Spain, seeking fabulous treasure, echoed back from its surface. The Comanches rode it, mounted on the "god-dog," as they called the horse.

From the Red River to the New Mexico territorial line it split Texas, ageless, inscrutable, voicing not the grim stories it could have told of bloodshed and death, of golden hopes and black despair — the Thunder Trail!

Through the pine forests of the east it ran, past slumbering bayous. Then across seemingly endless plains. Then, far to the southwest, with the pink and purple canyons of the Big Bend and the mountains and deserts of the trans-Pecos region, climbing and crossing the threatening loom of the Cap Rock and the zone of broken country below called "the breaks".

Always in the past it had been a "trail from yesterday," but now it was a "trail to tomorrow," for following almost exactly the path of those most precise surveyors, the buffalo, twin ribbons of steel were flowing westward, mile on mile of heartbreaking, back-breaking toil, to where the relentless ambition of an empire builder was cleaving a path through the granite of the mountains for those on-creeping ribbons of steel.

James G. "Jaggers" Dunn, the famed General Manager and driving force of the great C. & P. Railroad System, knew that this northern route would save many, many miles of rail travel and would tap new fields of production.

Others had said it couldn't be done, but in Jim Dunn's lexicon there was no such word as "couldn't." It *could* be done, he said, and he was proving the statement.

And now the Thunder Trail was really a trail of thunder. From the east sounded a mutter that loudened to a rumble, to the echoing crash of steel on steel. Something took form and shape; resolved into a great locomotive, stack purring, side rods clanking, which roared westward, quivering the air with such man-made thunder as the Spanish invader and riding Comanche never dreamed of.

Behind the iron monster rocked and swayed a long line of material and freight cars, heading for those western mountains, now not far off, and the brawling, bellowing construction camp, really the town of Redmon, that lay in the shadow of the mountain range.

2

Progress! Attended by turbulence, violence, bloodshed and death. But progress, the end justifying the means.

After the tumult and the shouting ceased would come prosperity, homes, happiness for the many.

So thought the lonely horseman sitting his tall black steed on the crest of a rise as he watched, with the eyes of vision and understanding, the train speed past.

Ranger Walt Slade, named by the Mexican *peons* of the Rio Grande river villages, *El Halcon* — The Hawk — raised his eyes to where a great dark smudge stained the clear blue of the Texas sky. Under that smudge lay Redmon, his destination.

"And, feller," he told Shadow, his great black horse, "guess we'd better jog along to that hell-raising pueblo if we wish to get there before dark. I'm in the notion of the nosebag, and I reckon you are, too. So June along, horse, we got things to do."

Shadow, sensing oats in the offing, snorted cheerful agreement and ambled down the rise to where, alongside the right of way, the going was good. Very quickly he picked up speed. Slade didn't curb him, for it had been a long time since breakfast, not much of a breakfast at that, and he too felt the need of a bite to eat.

East, south and north rolled the seemingly endless prairie. This was cattle land at its best, and here was a cattlemen's empire. Here the barons of the open range lived, many of them, in almost feudal splendor, regulating customs to their liking, a law unto themselves.

Some of them resented the coming of the railroad, although it would provide shorter and easier market drives, being opposed to all that spelt change. And they maintained, not without a modicum of truth, that the railroad would bring in riff-raff, owlhoots, and other undesirable characters.

That the ultimate good would outweigh all this, Walt Slade well knew, but it was offtimes difficult to persuade stubborn and opinionated individuals to see it that way.

Well, one of the reasons he was here was to do a little gentle "persuading". He chuckled as Shadow paced on, with the rumble of Redmon now reaching his amazingly sensitive ears, and with the smoke cloud growing darker and more ominous.

Half an hour later found him riding along what a signboard nailed to a post proclaimed to be Main Street.

The town was a sprawl of shacks, cabins, adobes, tents and false fronts. The better buildings, per usual, housed saloons. Slade paused before one, dismounted and dropped the split reins to the ground, which would keep Shadow where he was until called for.

Across the plate glass window was lettered in red the elegant pseudonym, "Crow Bait Corral." Slade entered, in quest of information; bartenders know everything.

The place was big and rather surprisingly well furnished, with an air of permanence to it. Which was not too surprising, for Redmon was very likely here to stay.

A pleasant-faced elderly drink juggler served him with a smile and a nod. As he sipped his drink, Slade asked a question;

"Can you direct me to Deputy Boone's office?"

"One block west, turn into Grand Avenue and you'll see a sign hanging in front of the door," replied the barkeep. " 'Spect you'll find Sheriff Ben Ord there, too; he spends more time here than he does at the county seat. Wouldn't be surprised if you find 'em sorta on the outs, especially with cowhands —" with a glance at Slade's rangeland garb.

"How come?" the Ranger asked.

"Bad shootin' in one of the rumholes over on Park Avenue," the bartender replied. "Railroad feller killed. Folks said some cowhands did it and they hightailed outa town 'fore the sheriff got a chance to grab 'em. Thought maybe you'd oughta know 'fore you maybe brace him for something."

"Thank you for your consideration," Slade replied as he shoved his empty glass aside. "I'll try not to rile him." His even teeth flashing white in a smile, he left the saloon. The bartender watched his tall form through the swinging doors.

"And," he remarked to the glass he was polishing, "if I was a sheriff or anything else, I sure wouldn't want to rile *him*. Not a jigger with eyes like he's got. Never saw such eyes! They go through you like a greased knife. Look right down inside of you and see what's there. And if there are any dark spots you'd sorta like to keep covered up, look out!"

5

Which went to indicate that the amiable drink juggler was no slouch when it came to reading men.

Outside, Slade motioned to Shadow. "Come along, jughead," he said. "Just an amble to Grand Avenue, and we'll take a chance on that bad-tempered sheriff. Grand Avenue! Park Avenue! Pueblo sure goes in for high sounding street names. Suppose the *Champs Elysées* will be right around the next corner."

Shadow declined to get into an argument about it and, after his master flipped up the reins, paced along composedly, to pause before the swinging sign that proclaimed "Sheriff's Office," where the reins were dropped again.

Lean, lanky and grizzled old Sheriff Ben Ord was in a bad temper, all right. He glowered up from his desk as Slade entered. Then he jumped to his feet with such alacrity as to knock over his chair.

"Well, blankety-blank, blank me for a sheepherder!" he whooped. "Where in blazes did *you* come from? So we've got El Halcon, the notorious owlhoot too smart to get caught, in our midst, eh? If I didn't have enough trouble!"

His craggy features split wide in a grin as he shook hands warmly.

"How are you, Walt?" he chuckled. "Sure fine to see you again. But how in blazes did you happen along at such a good time? I was figuring to write Captain McNelty a letter. In fact, I was just getting ready to. You musta been sorta inspired to show up like you have. How come, anyhow?"

Slade shook hands with Deputy Hal Boone before replying and then countered with a question of his own;

"Jim Dunn's here, isn't he?"

"That's right," replied Ord. "His private car is over in the yards. So he got in touch with McNelty, eh?"

"He did," Slade agreed. "They're old *amigos*, you know. He wired he was feeling sorry for you, that you were having trouble with sidewalk spitters and hellions turning over trash barrels and couldn't seem to make any headway against them, and he'd better send me along to lend a hand before you had a stroke."

"That spavined old coot!" Ord snorted indignantly. "He'll have a stroke when I get my hands on him. Seriously, though, Walt, Dunn is right, there is trouble."

"Okay," Slade said, "you can give me the details later. Right now I want to put up my horse and then tie onto something to eat."

"I'll take you to the stable where I keep my nag," Ord answered. "Good place. Only decent shacks in town are livery stables and rumholes. Then there's a place around on Main Street where they put out good chuck. You must have passed it; the Crow Bait Corral."

"Yes, I stopped there to ask where you were located," Slade replied. "Let's go. See you later, Hal."

"I'll squat here and keep an eye on things," said the deputy. "Something liable to bust loose any minute."

The stable, run by an old Mexican who bowed low to El Halcon and exclaimed over Shadow, proved satisfactory. Juan, the keeper, was formally introduced to Shadow, a one-man horse who allowed nobody to put a hand on him without his master's sanction, and led the big black to a stall.

"The rubdown, all, will cared for be," Juan told Slade. "Fear not, *Capitan*, the best get will he."

Satisfied that Shadow would be properly cared for, Slade thanked the old keeper in flawless Spanish and left him with smiles wreathing his wrinkled face.

Now the sunset was flaunting its gold and scarlet splendor over the mountain crests, while from deep in their granite bowels came intermittent rumblings.

"Day shift settin' off their blasts," said Ord, jerking his head in that direction. "Dunn is driving straight west. Hard going through that granite, but he says it'll give him a big advantage in his competition with the road down to the south of here. Will cut off miles of going. Figures that when this line is linked with other lines of his System, he'll tie onto most of the Chicago westbound trade. Guess he's right; he usually knows what he's talking about. He — what in blazes!"

Another rumbling boom had quivered the air, but not from the mountains. From nearby.

CHAPTER
TWO

"Dynamite, sure as heck!" exclaimed the sheriff. "It was over at the yards. Come on, right around the next corner!"

The corner was less than half a score of paces distant, but before they reached it, there was a clatter of hoofs and around the turn bulged five horsemen going like the wind.

A shout of alarm, a gleam of shifted metal — Slade hurled the sheriff from him, going sideways himself in the same ripple of movement.

A gun blazed. A bullet fanned his face. He whipped both his big Colts from their sheaths and let drive as the bunch swept past them, shooting wildly.

A man reeled in the saddle, slumped forward, almost fell, but grabbed the horn and kept his seat. The arm of another flew up, dropped to hang limp. Slade lined sights again as they swept around the next corner, with little hope of scoring a hit.

"You all right?" he anxiously asked the raving sheriff.

"Slug sliced the back of my hand, nothing to it," Ord replied, wringing the blood that dripped from his fingers. "Come on, let's see what happened."

They rounded the corner and the yards lay before them, some five hundred feet distant. A moment or two later they saw that smoke was pouring from the windows of a building, and a flicker of flame. A man was being carried out the door. Other men were running toward the blaze with buckets of water. Directing operations was a stocky, broad-shouldered individual with a glorious mane of crinkly white hair sweeping back from his big dome-shaped forehead. Slade strode up behind him and tapped him on the shoulder.

"How are you, Mr. Dunn?" he said.

Jaggers Dunn whirled around at the touch. His frosty blue eyes widened.

"Well, I'll be hanged!" he sputtered. "Slade! Got here at just the right time, per usual. Hello, Ord, now we'll get some action."

"Done got some," growled the sheriff, wringing the blood from his fingers again.

"What happened?" Slade asked.

"Hellions chucked a capped and fused stick of dynamite through the window as they rode past," Dunn replied.

"Some of Hans Ragnal's devils, I'll bet my last peso," declared Ord, with a growl.

"Could be," the G. M. admitted. " 'Pears nobody got a good look at them."

"Hat brims pulled down low, neckerchiefs pulled up high," Slade remarked. "Nothing much to be seen except their eyes, by the average observer."

Dunn shot him a quick look, for he well knew that El Halcon was *not* an average observer. It was said of his eyes that they could see around corners and through chunks of mountain. A slight exaggeration, no doubt, but not too far from the truth.

"You'd recognize them if you saw them again?" the G. M. muttered in low tones.

"I would," Slade replied. "Anybody badly hurt?"

"Guess not," Dunn replied. "Some of the boys cut and bruised a bit by flying glass and other debris, nothing serious. One fellow knocked out by the concussion, but I see he's coming out of it okay. Fortunately, there was nobody close to where the blast cut loose. Also fortunately, the two hundred or so boxes of dynamite that were on this side of the building, it's a storehouse, were moved to the other side before it happened. Otherwise there might be a nice crater where the shack was."

Slade stared at him. "Two hundred boxes of dynamite in a storehouse! Don't you have an underground storage for explosives?"

"Yep," Dunn replied, "but somebody slipped and the powder was put in here when it was unloaded. I spotted it just a little while ago and ordered it placed where it belonged. That's why it was moved from this side of the building, so the night yard men, who are just about due to take over, could shove it into the powder hole."

"I see," Slade said, his eyes thoughtful.

"You'll stay here tonight, of course," Dunn said, gesturing with his thumb toward a long green-and-gold splendor on a nearby spur. It was the Winona, General

11

Manager Dunn's palatial private car, known all over the great C. & P. System.

"Yes, I'll spend the night with you," Slade agreed.

"Okay," nodded Dunn. "Sam will take care of you no matter what time you show up. Here he comes now."

The elderly colored man, the G. M.'s combination porter and chef, came forward grinning widely as his eyes rested on El Halcon. They were old *amigos* and shook hands warmly.

"That's right, Mr. Slade," he said. "Your regular state-room, the one next to the front. Be all set, Mr. Slade."

"Thank you, Sam," the Ranger answered. "See you later, or in the morning, Mr. Dunn. And now, Ben, suppose we make another try for that surrounding; I'm beginning to feel a bit lank."

"Be glad to fix you a snack, Mr. Slade," Sam instantly offered.

"Thank you, Sam, but I believe I'd like to browse around for a little while," Slade declined. "Be seeing you too, later."

As they headed for the Crow Bait, Slade was silent, the concentration furrow deep between his black brows. Ord asked,

"What you thinking about, Walt? I know that look — you've got something on your mind."

"I was thinking," Slade replied, "that it is very, very fortunate those two hundred cases of dynamite were properly boxed and none of them open. Otherwise you might need a new town about now."

12

"By gosh! I never thought of that," Ord said. "It would have made quite a bang. A pity it didn't blow up those five sidewinders, though."

"If it all had let go, it very likely would have done that," Slade answered. "I think somebody erred a trifle and cut the fuse just a mite short. They were hardly in the clear when the stick exploded, that is in the clear so far as two hundred boxes are concerned. But it would have been a high price to pay for five worthless lives, in all likelihood. A hundred others might well have died."

"Guess that's right," the sheriff conceded. "Anyhow, you nicked a couple of the horned toads."

"Not too seriously, however, I fear," Slade said. "They, were able to keep going."

"Wonder why they threw down on us that way?" growled Ord. "You'd think they wouldn't have wanted to draw attention to themselves."

"Well," Slade pointed out, smiling slightly, "they could hardly have missed seeing that shield pinned to your shirt-front. They might have thought you planned to stop them, and right then they wouldn't have desired to be stopped by a law enforcement officer."

"Right once more," said the sheriff. He chuckled, and fished something from a pocket.

"Speaking of shields," he said, "here's your deputy sheriff's badge, the same one you wore when you were with me over at the county seat a couple of years back. I swore you in then, and I don't recall revoking your commission. Guess it's still in order."

Slade smiled, accepted the badge and dropped it in his own pocket. He had a premonition he would need it, and it would probably relieve him of the necessity of revealing his Ranger connections, which he preferred not to do, if possible.

"Well, here we are," said Ord. "Sorta empty right now. Guess everybody is over to the fire, but they'll be back."

The friendly bartender caught Slade's eye, smiled and nodded.

"How are you, Sheriff?" he greeted Ord. "The old thing, I reckon," evidently referring to the sheriff's customary tipple.

"Yep, send over a couple," replied Ord.

"I'll make mine coffee," Slade said. "Goes better on an empty stomach, and mine is sure empty right now."

"Everybody to their taste," the sheriff acceded cheerfully as they sat down and gave a waiter their order.

"Say!" he added. "Was so excited and worked up, it plumb slipped my mind. You took one helluva chance, shoving me in the clear 'fore you ducked yourself. Mighta got yourself plugged."

"Had to get you out of the way so I could line sights," Slade said with a smile. The sheriff snorted derisively.

"Anyhow, those devils got a lesson what it means to try and swap lead with the fastest gunhand in the whole dadblamed Southwest," he said. " 'Spect when they hear they were buckin' El Halcon, they'll make themselves sorta scarce hereabouts for a while."

"I doubt it," Slade differed. "Whoever they were, they struck me as the kind that doesn't scare easy. By the way, you mentioned a name; Hans Ragnal, I believe it was. What about him?"

"A cantankerous old shorthorn whose land, the Slash H, butts right up against the right-of-way, from the north. Got no use for the railroad and has been soundin' off plenty against it. Of course his riders, ornery, quarrelsome young galoots, follow his lead," the sheriff said.

"I see," Slade replied. "Same old story, doesn't go for progress, wants things to remain in the status quo. A prototype of old King Canute trying to sweep back the tide with a broom. Canute only succeeded in drowning himself; something similar could happen to Ragnal, if he doesn't change his viewpoint, recognize the inevitable, and adapt himself to changed conditions.

"However," he added meaningly, "don't go jumping at conclusions where Ragnal is concerned; no proof, so far as I have been able to ascertain from what Dunn wired Captain Jim, and what you have told me."

"Maybe not," conceded Ord, "but just the same I have my notions about that bunch."

"Okay, just so you don't go 'notioning' out loud," Slade smiled. "By the way, the bartender told me a man was killed last night, in a place over on Park Avenue, I believe he said."

"That's right," said Ord. "In one of those rumholes where you can't get anybody to talk. A railroad construction worker. All I could learn, from a bartender, was that he got into a ruckus with some cowhands and one of them plugged him. Barkeep said he never saw them before, which was what was to be

15

expected from a drink juggler in such a wind spider nest. The third killing this month."

"All railroad workers?"

"That's right. Who did it? Nobody knows, or if they do know, they ain't saying." Slade nodded, his eyes again thoughtful.

Now men were streaming into the Crow Bait, jabbering excitedly.

"I know darn well I heard shootin' right after that boom," a loud-mouthed individual was proclaiming. "Didn't see no carcasses layin' around, though."

"You're always seein' or hearin' something," said a companion. "Most of 'em out of a bottle. I didn't hear any shootin'."

"You're always runnin' off at the mouth so loud you can't hear anything 'cept your own spoutin'," declared the other.

"Looks like folks are sorta puzzled," Ord chuckled in low tones.

"Let them keep puzzling," Slade advised. "Just a chance it might cause somebody interested to drop a careless word."

"Right still another time," agreed the sheriff. "Well, here comes our chuck, about time. I'm ready to topple over."

Talk ceased for a while as the two peace officers addressed themselves to their food with appetite.

Finally the sheriff pushed back his empty plate and ordered a snort of redeye. Slade settled for more coffee and rolled a cigarette.

"Say," he remarked, glancing around, "this place is doing a business."

"Yes, it is, the best in town and gets the best crowd," said Ord. "That sorta old jigger who told you where to find me — he's down at the far end of the bar by the till and the back room, now — is Mack Ware, the owner. A good man and a squareshooter. He runs his place strictly on the up-and-up, and it pays off. More than you can say for most of the pack rat nests in this blasted hell-town. Mack says that if you treat folks right, they'll usually treat you right.

"Yep, he's a nice, quiet-spoke jigger, but he can be plenty salty if necessary. Got a couple of floor men of the same sort. Play it square. Goes for his barkeeps and his dealers, and for his girls. Here *they* come now, onto the dance floor. Not bad?"

"Decidedly not," Slade agreed, his glance appreciative.

The girls were indeed young and pretty, some of them dark-eyed little *señoritas* of the best class.

"Mack brought 'em with him from a place he had over east," Ord observed. "Same goes for his other help. He says this pueblo is here to stay and that it'll quiet down after the construction work moves ahead."

"He's right on both counts," Slade said. "The site is a natural, now that rail facilities will be available, and most of the rowdy element will move along with the construction; there'll be another camp west of the mountains and they'll flock to that, leaving the more substantial folks here as permanent settlers. Has happened in other sections of Texas, and elsewhere.

"Incidentally," he added a moment later, "that Mexican orchestra he has can really play. Did he bring them along, too?"

"Brought 'em up from down around Laredo," Ord replied. "You know those fellers are just like chuck line riders, always on the move, and glad to coil their twine in a new diggin's, for a while. Wouldn't be surprised if you know some of 'em, seeing as you spent quite a bit of time around Laredo."

"I thought their faces looked familiar," Slade interpolated.

"Quite a few miles to Laredo," Ord resumed, "but not a bad trip, 'cause, with a coupla changes, all except the last forty miles or so can be made by train. As you know, of course, Dunn never misses a bet and brought the telegraph wires right along with his steel, so he can keep in touch with his Chicago office and the rest of the world, and we have an office here. So the boys wired Mack and he had an equipage waiting for them when they left the train. They could have hired one, or horses, if need be, of course. And here they are.

"And," he added with a chuckle, "they've recognized you, too. Look at the leader bendin' his back!"

The orchestra leader was indeed bowing low to El Halcon. Slade waved his hand in acknowledgement of the courtesy, and six pairs of hands waved back.

"I'll go over and have a word with them," he said.

Reaching the little raised platform, he shook hands with the musicians and engaged them in conversation.

"Does *Capitan* hope to remain long?" the leader asked.

18

"For quite a while, I expect," Slade admitted. "At least until the railroad gets through the mountains."

"*Bueno! Bueno!*" exclaimed the leader.

"*Gracias*," El Halcon replied.

Ord's gaze was fixed on the Ranger as he lounged gracefully beside the platform.

"Golly! What a fine looking young feller he is," he murmured to himself. He was right.

CHAPTER
THREE

Walt Slade was very tall, more than six feet, the breadth of his shoulders and the depth of his chest matching his splendid height.

His face was as striking as his form. A rather wide mouth, grin-quirked at the corners, somewhat relieved the fierceness evinced by the prominent hawk nose above and the powerful jaw and chin beneath. His pushed-back "J.B." disclosed a broad forehead surmounted by crisp, thick black hair.

The sternly handsome countenance was dominated by long, black-lashed eyes of very pale gray. Cold reckless eyes that nevertheless always seemed to have little devils of laughter lurking in their clear depths. But did those devils abruptly leap to the front, they would be anything but laughing; then the normally kindly eyes, despite their coldness, would become the "terrible eyes of El Halcon," most disquieting to anyone upon whom they chanced to rest.

Slade wore the homely garb of the rangeland — Levi's, the bibless overalls favored by the cowhands, soft blue shirt with vivid neckerchief looped at the throat, half-boots of softly tanned leather — and he wore it as gallant Coronado must have worn steel or velvet.

Encircling his sinewy waist were double cartridge belts, from the carefully oiled and worked cut-out holsters of which protruded the plain black butts of heavy guns.

And from those gun butts, his slender, muscular hands seemed never far away.

After a few more words with the musicians, Slade rejoined the sheriff, who remarked,

"Those jiggers are up to something; look at them!"

On the platform, heads had drawn together in low-voiced conversation. White teeth flashed in grins. The leader disengaged himself from the group and hurried across to where Mack Ware stood at the end of the bar. More talk ensued. Ware also grinned, and nodded. He drew a sheet of paper from a drawer and wrote several lines on it, the leader nodding approval. Calling a floor man, Ware handed him the paper, the grin broadening. The floor man also grinned, and hurried out. Ware glanced toward Slade and his grin widened still more. Evidently chuckling, he turned back to the bar.

"Now what are those hellions up to?" Slade wondered.

"I don't know," replied Ord, "but I betcha *you'll* find out."

"I don't doubt but you're right," Slade conceded. "And I don't trust them one bit; they have a perfectly reprehensible sense of humor. Well, guess all I can do is wait and see."

However, whatever was in the wind was not translated into action, at least for the time being. A little later the floor man returned, nodded to Ware. He did not glance in Slade's direction, nor did Ware, nor did the musicians.

"Now what?" the sheriff asked.

"Another cup of coffee while I finish my cigarette and then suppose we browse about a bit," Slade suggested. "I'd like to have a look at some other places, especially that one on Park Avenue where the railroad worker was killed."

"A good notion," Ord agreed. "I'll have another snort while I'm waiting." Which he proceeded to do.

"By the way," Slade remarked, "I wonder where I can tie onto a room? I'll sleep at Dunn's car tonight, but I want a place where I can hole up permanently while I'm here."

"Right upstairs," replied the sheriff. "I know Ware has a couple he rents out to the right people. This is one of the few two-story shacks in town, and one of the biggest. Ware had it built to his own way of thinking. One or two of the dealers sleep up there, and one of the floor men and a bartender, and some of the girls. Reckon you won't be bothered too much, or can put up with it."

"Don't see why I should be," Slade said smilingly.

"Oh, dealers and bartenders sometimes make a racket going upstairs," the sheriff explained innocently. "I'll go speak to Ware."

He did so, and returned with a couple of keys, which he passed to Slade.

"Little one is to the second room to the right from the head of the stairs," he said. "Big one is to the outside door that leads to the stairs."

Slade thanked him and pocketed the keys. Waving goodnight to Ware, they left the Crow Bait.

The Crow Bait was noisy and boisterous, but the streets were worse, jam-packed by a jostling, bellowing throng. There were railroaders, construction workers, some Mexicans, cowhands. The board sidewalks quivered to the thud of boots; dust swirled from under the hoofs of cow ponies. There were dance floor girls, out for a breath of fresh air. Other girls, apparently out for most anything. Some were escorted; others, who were not, cast languishing glances at the tall Ranger.

So far, things were peaceful enough. But the night was young and later, when the redeye began really getting in its licks, conditions would very likely change, and for the worse.

Slade paid the crowd little mind. He was not here to quiet drunken roisterers, but to run down certain vicious robbers and killers who preyed on the irresponsible workers and honest businessmen.

Sheriff Ord jerked his thumb toward a set of swinging doors.

"That place was robbed last week," he said. "Bartender killed. A rather nice jigger, from all accounts. Nobody safe in this blasted snake hole. Right around the next corner and we'll drop in at that place where the railroader was killed last night, the Comstock."

Slade nodded, and noticed a man turning the corner just ahead of them, glancing back over his shoulder. As he and the sheriff turned the corner, he spotted the fellow walking swiftly. Twice he glanced back over his shoulder, and each time increased his pace a little. Slade lengthened his stride a bit, the sheriff mechanically keeping up with him.

Ahead, the man glanced back for still a third time, ducked between swinging doors next to an expanse of plate glass legended COMSTOCK. Slade reached up and loosened his hat's chin strap.

They reached the swinging doors, turned toward them.

"Keep behind me," Slade snapped to Ord. He reached up again, flipped his hat. It went sailing over the swinging doors. Slade bounded after it, hurling the doors wide open.

Near the end of the bar stood three men, staring at the hat on the floor. They glanced up. One of them yelped,

"Look out!"

Slade's hands flickered down and up as the three went for their holsters. The room fairly exploded to the bellow of gunfire.

Weaving, ducking, Slade shot with both hands, and again. One of the trio reeled sideways and fell. Another rocked back on his heels, slumped to the floor. The third wheeled and fled, knocking men right and left, and tore through the open door of a back room. Slade tried to line sights but dared not squeeze triggers because there were men between him and the racing

24

target and they might well stop lead. In the back, a door banged open and shut.

It had all happened so swiftly that for a moment the crowd stood stunned. And as a whirl of exclamations started to rise, Slade's great voice rolled in thunder through the room,

"Hold it! As you are! Excitement all over!"

The smoking muzzles of his big Colts, weaving back and forth, emphasized the command. The tumult stilled, even the dance floor girls mouthing back their shrieks.

And now the sheriff, sputtering profanity, was beside El Halcon, gun in hand and looking like he'd welcome a chance to use it.

Satisfied everything was under control, Slade strode forward and paused beside the two bodies.

"Thought so," he remarked to Ord. "Two of the dynamiters. Didn't waste much time trying to even the score."

"Grimshaw!" bawled the sheriff, waving his cocked gun, to the accompaniment of gentlemen discreetly ducking out of line. "Grimshaw! Where the hell are you? Come here!"

A bullet-headed fellow with a scared face came hurrying to him.

"I didn't have anything to do with it, Sheriff," he babbled. "I didn't know what those devils were up to. The two of 'em were standin' by the bar when the other one came bustin' in and said something. They all faced the door, but looked down when that hat came sailin' in. That feller won't have any more to say; that's him layin' on his back."

"One more caper like this and I'll close this rumhole so tight it'll take a locomotive to open it," Ord promised, glowering at the scared owner. "A killing last night, and a try at murder tonight! I think I *will* close it."

"Please don't, Sheriff," Grimshaw pleaded. "I'll try and keep better order from now on. I didn't have any way of knowin' those horned toads meant trouble."

"Guess he's right," Slade interpolated, slanting a meaningful glance at the sheriff, who growled and swore but said nothing more.

"Where does that back door lead to?" Slade asked.

"Reckon you'd call it an alley," Grimshaw replied. "Dark out there."

"Suppose we take a look," Slade suggested to the sheriff.

"A notion," Ord agreed.

Slade opened the door cautiously and shot a quick glance in every direction, although he thought there was little chance the fugitive gunman would be lurking somewhere in the darkness.

Enough light filtered into the alley to show it was deserted save two horses tethered to a protruding beam.

"Didn't think he'd take time to loose them," Slade said. "Let's lead them into the light and look them over."

It was done. Slade glanced at the brands.

"Altered burns and mean nothing," he said. "Good-looking critters, though. Should bring enough to pay for the funeral."

"And wouldn't be surprised if those two devils have some in their pockets, too," Ord predicted hopefully. "Say! That hat trick of yours was something! How'd you catch on?"

"Their lookout who was keeping tabs on us made a mistake," Slade explained. "I thought it a trifle strange that he should keep looking back over his shoulder at us and speeding up a bit each time, as if he desired to reach some place before we did. When he ducked into the Comstock, what was in the making was fairly plain. I thought the hat ambling in first would distract their attention long enough for me to get into action, were something really lined up. They were all set to mow us down when we stepped in the door. Didn't work."

"It sure didn't," chortled Ord. "Is there ever anything you don't think of?"

"Plenty," Slade smiled, "but that set-up was fairly obvious. Well, we might as well get back inside. I don't think we'll have any more action tonight."

"Hope not," grumbled Ord. "This sort of thing is hard on the nerves. What is it, Grimshaw?"

"I suppose you'll want those bodies packed to your office, Sheriff?" the owner said ingratiatingly. "I'll have my boys take care of the chore."

"Much obliged," replied the sheriff. "Deputy Boone will be there; he'll look after them. Ever see them before?"

Grimshaw shook his head. So did others who were listening. Which did not surprise Slade. He had already concluded that the Comstock habitues were not given to loose talking that might involve them in unpleasant consequences.

"After we look them over, I'm heading for the yards," Slade announced as they followed the body packers along Park Avenue. "Dunn will be wondering what has become of me."

"He won't worry, knowing you as he does," Ord predicted confidently. "He'll just be wondering what happened to somebody else. Well! Well! Not a bad day, after all two hellions got their comeuppance and a couple more nicked, with just a scratch on the back of my hand to chalk up against our side. Pueblo will be humming about El Halcon tonight. You've been recognized, of course."

"Quite likely," Slade conceded with a smile. "Folks come here from all over and it is possible somebody recalls me as El Halcon from elsewhere."

Personally, he thought it probable but was little concerned with the possibility.

"That blasted El Halcon business worries me, just as it worried Jim McNelty," grumbled the sheriff. "Oh, I know, as El Halcon you get to hear things you wouldn't if everybody knew you to be a Ranger. And owlhoots figuring you to be just one of their own bunch hornin' in on good things they've got started sometimes get a mite careless, and pay for it. But I'm always scairt some loco deputy or marshal will take a shot at you on general principles, and you'd be sorta at a disadvantage 'cause you wouldn't want to kill a peace officer.

Chances are, though, you'd wing him before he could get into action, and then explain.

"And there's a chance, too, that some professional gun slinger wanting to be known as the jigger who downed the fastest gunhand in the whole Southwest might take a try at pluggin' you in the back. But the chances are he'd just tie onto six feet of earth four feet down. But it does worry me."

Because of his habit of working undercover whenever possible and not revealing his Ranger connections, Slade had tied onto a peculiar two-sided reputation. Some people who knew him only as El Halcon with killings to his credit insisted he was just an owlhoot himself, so far too smart to get caught. Others who also knew him only as El Halcon were his vigorous defenders, pointing out that he worked on the side of law and order with reputable sheriffs who weren't easy to fool.

Those who knew the truth, like Sheriff Ord, declared him to be not only the most fearless but also the ablest of the Rangers.

And the Mexican *peones* and other humble folks would say.

"El Halcon! the good, the just, the compassionate, the friend of the lowly! May *El Dios* ever guard him!"

Which meant more to Slade than all else. So despite the fact that it *did* worry him, Captain Jim McNelty, the famous Commander of the Border Battalion of the Texas Rangers, did not forbid the deception, and Slade went his careless way as El Halcon and worried about the possible consequences not at all.

CHAPTER
FOUR

When they reached the office they found the two bodies laid out on the floor with Deputy Boone keeping an eye on them. Ord went through their pockets but turned out nothing Slade considered of significance save a good sum of money which would go to enrich the county treasury.

But the seams of the pockets did interest the Ranger, who examined them carefully, his black brows drawing together. Straightening up, he gazed out the window for a moment, then sat down and rolled a cigarette with the slim fingers of his left hand. After finishing the smoke, he said goodnight to Ord and headed for the railroad yards.

When he reached the private car, he found Dunn sitting up in the drawing room, which served as an office, smoking a cigar. He waved Slade to a chair and called to Sam to bring coffee and a snack.

"Any more excitement?" he asked.

Slade recounted, briefly, the affair at the Comstock. The magnate listened with interest, nodding his big head from time to time.

"So, didn't waste any time trying to even up the score, eh?" he remarked when the Ranger paused.

"I don't think that was the idea," Slade replied.

"No?"

"No, I think somebody is anxious to eliminate me, feeling that I am in his way," Slade said. Dunn continued to nod.

"Yes, it could be that," he conceded. "Has happened before when you were with me. Well, I'm not overly surprised. You have a little habit of getting in the way of gents who are trying to finagle some undercover scheme. No, coming on top of other things that have happened of late, I wouldn't be a bit surprised."

"Been having trouble, I understand," Slade remarked.

"Yes, we have," Dunn admitted. "Quite a few things been pulled. A steam shovel blown to smithereens. A lead switch that shouldn't have been was open. Result, a material train plowed into a string of cars. Nice pile-up it took a couple of days to clear. Fortunately nobody killed. But a man was killed by a premature dynamite explosion. The worst thing about such incidents, they slow up the work, for after a while the men get jumpy and don't perform with their usual efficiency."

"Anybody you suspect as being responsible?" Slade asked. Dunn hesitated a moment,

"Well," he said at length, "some of the cattlemen of the section resent the coming of the road. There's that fellow Ragnal whom Ord no doubt mentioned to you. He's a big owner, one of the biggest hereabouts, and he's been fighting us tooth and nail. Tried to lay claim to the land over which the right of way passes. Courts threw that out, which I expect made him still madder. And there are others of the same calibre. Same old

31

story, the old jiggers who have always run things to their liking don't want change."

"Could be it," Slade conceded. "Although it seems a trifle unreasonable they would risk a penitentiary sentence or a hanging to vent their spleen. Of course, under such circumstances, hired hands sometime jump over the traces and commit acts their employers wouldn't countenance. That has happened."

He paused to sip the coffee Sam brought and for a few minutes sat gazing at the dark window square opposite him. Then abruptly he asked a question.

"How about your M. K. *amigos?* They're building a line west only about fifty miles south of here, and your line will have many miles of advantage over them and will tap new fields of business they have hoped to get. And I suppose there are some lucrative mail and express contracts also involved."

"Right on both counts," Dunn returned. "As to whether they might be mixed up in the business I don't know. Since you put the fear of God in them with that Presidio business a while back, they've laid off. But they might be going into action again."

The M. K. was a rival system, the controlling interests of which were not noted for hewing close to the line where ethics were concerned. Jaggers Dunn had been feuding with them for years and recently, with Walt Slade's assistance, had come out very much on top.

"Well, anyhow I'm not worrying too much, now that I've got the best engineer in Texas lending me a hand," Dunn said.

Slade laughed. "Very complimentary, sir," he said, "but I fear you are prone to exaggeration."

"I ain't much on paying compliments and I don't tend to exaggerate," Dunn declared sturdily. "I merely recognize the truth when I see it."

"Thank you, sir," Slade smiled, and changed the subject.

"Have you any proof, sir, that the man Ragnal was involved in the depredations committed?" he asked.

"Nope," Dunn replied, "but some of his cowhands have been seen riding around and past the yards and the cutting, looking things over."

"Conceding that Ragnal is involved, he would not be likely to use his riders for such a chore, because of the danger of recognition," Slade pointed out.

"Could have brought in some scalawags to do his dirty work for him, couldn't he?" the G. M. countered.

"It has been done," Slade had to admit. "And in some instances the characters have gotten completely out of hand. Which is an angle that must be given consideration, but until something definite is proven against Ragnal he must be regarded only as a possible suspect. I'll have Ben Ord try and arrange a meeting with him before I attempt to arrive at any conclusion."

"That's reasonable, and the right thing to do," Dunn agreed. "And I repeat, now that I've got the top Ranger and the best engineer in Texas lined up, I ain't worrying."

Jaggers Dunn was not too far off in his somewhat startling statement. Shortly before the death of his father, which occurred after financial reverses that entailed the loss of the elder Slade's ranch, young Walt had graduated with high honors from a noted college of engineering. He had intended to take a postgraduate course in special subjects to better fit him for the profession he planned to make his life's work.

However, this became out of the question for the time being and he was somewhat at loose ends. So when Captain Jim McNelty, his father's friend, with whom Walt had worked some during summer vacations, suggested he come into the Rangers for a while and pursue his studies in spare time, Slade thought the idea a good one. Future events proved it was.

So Walt Slade became a Texas Ranger. Long since he had gotten more from private study than he could have hoped for from the postgrad. But meanwhile he had become enamoured of Ranger work. It provided so many opportunities to right wrongs and help the deserving. So although he had received offers of lucrative employment from titans of the business world, including Jaggers Dunn himself, Walt Slade was still a Ranger. Later he would become an engineer, but for a while yet he would stick with the Rangers.

Dunn glanced at the clock. "Getting late," he said.

"It is," Slade agreed. "And tomorrow I'd like to ride to the cutting and look things over."

"We'll do that," Dunn said. "So now I guess we'd better hit the hay. Just a minute, though. I might be called away from here in a hurry most any time, some deals pending, so we'd better provide against eventualities; never can tell what may bust loose in this blasted section."

He fished a letterhead from a drawer, wrote a few lines and appended his unmistakable "barbed wire" signature.

"Here you are," he said, passing the sheet to El Halcon. "Same as you've had before."

Slade received the paper and read,

To all officers and employees of the C. & P. Railroad System:— Orders given by the bearer, Walter J. Slade, are to be obeyed without question, to the letter, and at once.

"Guess that'll hold you," Jaggers said cheerfully as Slade folded and pocketed the document. "Now for a little shut-eye."

After a long and somewhat tempestuous day, Slade slept soundly and did not awaken until midforenoon.

"Boss Man said you wasn't to be disturbed," Sam explained as he set forth his breakfast. "He's out in the yards looking over some new machinery. Said to tell you he'd be back 'fore long, to take it easy and wait for him. Everything you want, sir? Plenty more hot coffee on the stove. Just let out a beller if you need something."

With a smile and a nod he ambled back to his kitchen. Slade attacked his meal with the appetite of youth and perfect digestion. He was settling back comfortably with a cup of steaming coffee and a cigarette when the railroad magnate arrived demanding nourishment, which Sam proceeded to provide.

"After I eat, suppose we ride over to the cutting," he suggested.

"A good idea," Slade agreed. "I'd like to have a look at things there."

After Dunn had put away his snack, they saddled their nags and set out for the cutting, which was less than a mile distant. Slade studied the terrain with the interest of the trained geologist.

Where the railroad was driving west was a long ridge, much lower than the surrounding crests and sliced by a deep notch that formed something very much in the nature of a pass. Under this notch the cutting bored through the ridge. A trail ran up the gentle slope to disappear into the notch, which was fairly broad.

"Another quarter mile or less and we drive a tunnel," Dunn remarked. "Will be a bit long, as tunnels go, a half mile and a little more, but should be easy going once we get past the granite casing."

"Should not pose any great difficulty," Slade replied. "A routine chore, I'd say, that is if everything is handled as it should be. Such an undertaking is tricky, however. Let somebody figure just a mite wrong and be off in his estimates and there's trouble in the making."

"And that's the reason I was so darned anxious to get you here if it was humanly possible," Dunn said. "If something is not just as it should be, you'll spot it, no doubt in my mind as to that. Ready to bet my last peso on it."

36

"Careful," Slade laughed. "Don't go off the deep end or you may end up eating snowballs."

"I ain't worrying," Dunn cheerfully repeated his former remark.

Shortly they reached the scene of operations. Here all was bustling activity. Picks thudded, shovels scraped, spike mauls banged. Steam shovels moved earth and chunks of rock. Air compressors chattered and drills bit into the stubborn granite. Charges of explosive were tamped into place. The air quivered to shouted orders.

A big man whose dark hair was sprinkled with gray came hurrying to meet them.

"Walt," Dunn said, "this is Morris Thomas, the engineer in charge of the project. Thomas, shake hands with Walt Slade. I expect he'll be around every now and then. You may have heard of him."

"Guess everybody has, after what happened yesterday," Thomas replied with a smile. He reached up his hand. Slade leaned over and they shook.

Thomas had a straight-featured face with a firm mouth. His eyes were big and dark, frank-looking, but with now and then an uncertain expression in the corners of them, Slade thought.

"Know anything about railroad building, Mr. Slade?" he asked with another smile.

"A little," the Ranger admitted, smiling in turn. Dunn chuckled.

With a wave of his hand he dismissed the engineer and they rode on a little farther.

"A good man," Dunn said, jerking his head toward Thomas. "Was with me on other projects, in a subordinate capacity. I decided he was the man for here."

Slade nodded but did not comment. He was studying the cutting, his black brows drawing together slightly.

For a while they watched operations, until Dunn remarked.

"Guess we've seen about everything there is to see. Now what?"

"I'd like to ride up the ridge and to the other side of the notch," Slade replied. "Want to have a look at it."

Dunn slanted him a glance but asked no questions. They left the cutting and rode up the winding trail, which pursued a straight line through the notch. They had covered less than a mile when they reached the west slope, which, similar to the east slope, was also long and gentle.

Reining in his horse, Slade studied the terrain. The slope, he estimated, was somewhat longer and even more gentle than the eastern slope. And on and on, toward the shadowy mountains of New Mexico, flowed the shallow depression which was the Thunder Trail.

Slade noted that but a few hundred yards to the north, a good sized stream which apparently had its inception at the base of the cliffs that flanked the ridge meandered westward, almost paralleling the ancient Thunder Trail.

There were certain other geological phenomena that interested the Ranger, which he put in the back of his mind for future reference, and which caused him to decide he'd pay another visit to the area sometime in the near future.

As he gazed toward the stream, the concentration furrow deepened between his black brows. A sure sign, Jaggers Dunn knew, that El Halcon was doing some thinking. But again he asked no questions, also knowing that Walt Slade would talk when he was ready to, not before.

With a last look down the slope and across the level prairie beyond, noting that the mountains jutted out for several miles on each side of the ridge, Slade said,

"Guess we might as well head back to the car."

"Well, what do you think?" Dunn asked as they turned their horses.

"I'll talk to you later, after I've done a little figuring," El Halcon replied.

However, he was to be deprived of the opportunity to discuss matters with the empire builder. As they neared the private car, Sam was on the back steps, waving an envelope.

"Telegram, Boss Man," he said. "Just come."

Dunn tore open the envelope, read the message and swore.

"I've got to head for Chicago right away," he said. "I'm needed there. Don't know how long I'll be tied up. So keep an eye on things till I get back. And you are in charge if you decide it is needful for you to be. The cooks, who are Mexicans, will take care of all your wants. Over at the cutting is the barracks we built for the boys, although they spend most of their non-working time in the blasted town. Have a shack built for your accommodation, over there or here, if you wish to."

"I think I'll hang onto my room over the Crow Bait Corral," Slade replied. "After all, I'm supposed to be a deputy sheriff, and when the chips are down, I *am* a Texas Ranger. But I'll look after your darn railroad. Don't be surprised if I make a few changes."

"You're in charge," Jaggers repeated, "so go to it and do anything you consider advisable. Be seeing you."

Twenty minutes later, a big locomotive boomed east with the private car, Dunn and old Sam waving goodbye from the rear platform. Slade stabled his horse and repaired to the sheriff's office in a very thoughtful frame of mind.

CHAPTER
FIVE

The sheriff wasn't in. So Slade sat down at his desk and began covering a sheet of paper with figures and symbols. After a while he studied the result for some minutes, then crumpled the sheet into a ball and tossed it in the waste-basket. For a few minutes he sat gazing out the window at the busy street. Then, with a shrug of his broad shoulders, he fished out the "makin's" and rolled and lighted a cigarette.

"Well," he said to the glowing tip, "looks like we have dropped right into the middle of something we didn't expect. But I have a very strong notion that it will tie up with what we are really here for. So hew to the line and hope to clip out some chips. Which is a rather original rendering of an old adage, don't you think?"

The tip was not responsive, so Slade flicked off the ashes with his little finger and took a deep drag.

Sheriff Ord rolled in a little later, looking expectant. He nodded to Slade and ambled into the back room to put coffee on to heat.

"Well, how did you and Dunn make out?" he asked when he returned.

"Okay," Slade replied. "He just left for Chicago."

"Hmmm!" said the sheriff. "Guess that means you'll be hanging around the construction work a bit, eh?"

"It is possible," Slade replied smilingly. "But that won't interfere with my other activities. In fact I've a notion it will promote them."

"Knowing you as I do, I figure it will," said Ord.

"Things quiet?" Slade asked.

"Quiet as they ever are in this snake nest," replied the sheriff. "At least no bad trouble so far today, but there's still plenty of time."

However, the sheriff's pessimism was not justified. Aside from the usual racket and hurly-burly, the day and the night passed peacefully enough. Mid morning found Slade riding to the cutting. Reaching the scene of operations, he dismounted. Thomas, the engineer, spotted him at once and approached to greet him.

"Well, what do you think of it?" he asked.

El Halcon did not answer the question. Instead, he asked one of his own;

"Mr. Thomas, you have a plat of the cutting and tunnel survey?"

"Why, yes, in my office," the engineer replied.

"Could I see it?"

"Why, certainly, if you wish," Thomas agreed, looking bewildered.

He led the way to the office and from a drawer produced the plat in question and handed it to the Ranger.

For several minutes, Slade studied it carefully, then handed it back and said,

"Just as I thought. The survey was incorrectly run, the estimates badly miscalculated. Follow that thing and thousands and thousands of dollars would be wasted and, which is more important, there would be added distance and a loss of time, for much of the work would have to be done over. The cutting grade must be reduced by three percent, the tunnel veered twenty degrees to the south."

The engineer's face flushed darkly red. His eyes sparkled, and he looked very angry.

"Mr. Slade," he snapped, "you are badly mistaken. With the help of Mr. Graham, my assistant and mathematician, I ran that survey myself and it is right."

Slade regarded him a moment before replying. Thomas tried to continue to look indignant, but the steadfast gaze of the pale, cold eyes caused him to shift uneasily in his chair. Slade spoke.

"Mr. Thomas," he said, "I give you credit for an honest mistake. But it is a mistake that must be rectified, and at once."

The engineer bristled. "Mr. Slade," he replied, "who are you to tell me what to do? I am in charge here."

In answer, Slade handed him Jaggers Dunn's terse directory. Thomas stared at it. His anger changed to utter bewilderment.

"Does — does this mean I am dismissed?" he faltered.

"It does not," Slade assured him. "You are to carry on as usual; Mr. Dunn has confidence in you. It merely means just what it implies, that *I* am in charge here, or anyplace else on the C. and P. System, for that matter, and I expect my orders to be obeyed at once."

Thomas raised his eyes from the paper, shrugged his shoulders.

"Okay," he said, "I'll follow instructions. Nobody argues with Mr. Dunn.

"And," he murmured to himself under his breath, "I've a notion nobody argues with *you* if he hankers to stay healthy!"

Slade smiled for the first time during the interview. "Pencil and paper, please," he requested.

The decidedly befuddled engineer supplied them. Again figures and symbols flowed beneath Slade's slender fingers. An equation took form, and another, and the solutions. With a final check of the figures, he passed the paper to Thomas who took it mechanically and studied it. Finally he looked up and met Slade's eyes.

"Mr. Slade," he said, "I owe you an apology. You are right. How we came to make such a blunder I cannot conceive. But we did, there is no doubt about it."

At that moment a man loomed in the doorway, glancing questioningly at El Halcon.

"Hello, Neale," Thomas greeted. "Come in. Mr. Slade, this is Neale Graham, my assistant and mathematician. Neale, meet the new Big Boss. He has saved us a lot of trouble; I hate to think of what Mr. Dunn would have had to say."

Graham was a big man, nearly as big as Thomas, but leaner. His coloring was lighter than Thomas's, his hair on the sandy side, his eyes light blue. Slade estimated his age at under forty, a few years younger than his superior. Slade thought him rather ruggedly good-looking.

Thomas waved him to a chair after he and Slade had shaken hands, and explained the situation. Graham accepted the paper on which Slade had worked and studied it for some moments, his eyes narrowing. He raised them to meet Slade's gaze.

"I see," he said. "The first solution represents the plan under which we have been working, the second the revised plan. Yes, Mr. Slade is right. I guess we were too eager to get started on the project and slipped. No use trying to explain it, for explanations never really explain. Then you, Mr. Slade, you have indeed saved us from trouble with Mr. Dunn."

Thomas rose to his feet. "Going out and line up the boys," he said. "Come along, Mr. Slade?"

Slade decided to do so and they left the office together. Graham remained, the paper containing. Slade's revised estimates in his hand.

Outside, Thomas beckoned a man who was giving orders to the workers. He was introduced as Terence Flaherty, the head foreman. Thomas outlined the change of plans. Slade thought that Flaherty did not appear particularly surprised. He put the big Irishman in the back of his mind for future reference.

The foreman began bellowing orders. Satisfied that everything was under control, for the present at least, Slade said goodbye to Thomas and Graham, mounted his horse and headed for Redmon.

"Shadow," he remarked, "outlandishly paraphrasing Shakespeare, there appears to be something fishy in

Texas. It seems inconceivable that two experienced engineers should make such a blunder. But such things have happened, so we'll hold our judgment in abeyance until we learn a little more. Let's go, horse; getting late, and about time for the nosebag."

Meanwhile the two engineers were holding a conference.

"What do you think of him?" Thomas asked.

"Dunn's trouble-shooter, of course," Graham replied. "Wouldn't be surprised if he's been with him for a long time. That deputy sheriff business is just a cover-up."

"Well, he sure knows his business," Thomas said. "He wasn't in that cutting yesterday for half an hour, and he had everything at his fingertips."

"Yes, he does," Graham agreed soberly. "Well, I take the blame for what happened, seeing as I did the figuring. One of those things that sometimes happen when one is working under forced draft, as we have been."

"The Old Man is in such a helluva hurry to get the line through and headed west," Thomas observed. "Well, we'll do it, now that we are on the right track, if the blasted cattlemen will just leave us alone. Maybe Slade can put a few bugs in a few ears there; I've a notion he is capable of it."

"Wouldn't be surprised if he is," Graham nodded. "A bad man to have against one."

"Yes," Thomas said, the uncertain look in the corners of his eyes intensifying.

When Slade reached the sheriff's office, he found Ord there. Without preamble he gave the sheriff a detailed account of his experience with the engineers.

46

"And what do you think?" Ord asked.

"Frankly, I hardly know what to think," Slade admitted. "It appears to be a ridiculous mistake, but such things have happened. They may have underestimated the thickness of the granite rind on which they propose to lay the roadbed. All this region was once highly volcanic, because of which peculiar geological phenomena are now and then encountered."

"Looks like Dunn would have noticed," the sheriff observed.

"Mr. Dunn is neither an engineer nor a geologist," Slade pointed out. "To properly evaluate conditions here he would need to be both."

"Guess that's so," Ord conceded. "Well, the coroner is coming over from the county seat to hold an inquest on those carcasses on the floor. Should be here shortly. Just a waste of time, but I figure he hankers for a night here. He ain't young anymore, but he's still got a twinkle in his eye. You remember him, of course; Doc Clay."

"Yes, I remember him," Slade replied. "A fine old jigger. Surprised to learn he's still here. He's just like McChesney, and Beard, and Cooper, and the rest of those old frontier practitioners, can't stay in one place overlong; known all over Texas, and elsewhere. I'll be glad to see him."

"Figured you would be," said Ord. "That's why I sent him word of what we had in stock. Otherwise we'd have just dug a hole and dumped 'em in."

"Flouting the law, eh?" Slade smiled. "Hardly the proper thing for a peace officer to do."

47

"Some loco laws need floutin'," growled Ord.

A little later, Dr. Sam Clay arrived, and trailing him was a coroner's jury he had collected on the way. His hair was white, his face wrinkled, but his eyes were wonderfully bright and youthful. He and Slade had a warm greeting for each other.

Doc quickly got down to business. The inquest was brief. The verdict rendered, which 'lowed the two outlaws got what was coming to them, surprised nobody. Court adjourned.

After a period of jabber, Slade, Doctor Sam and Sheriff Ord adjourned to the Crow Bait Corral for a snort or two and a surrounding.

Another night passed peacefully, at least with the kind of peace that was normal for Redmon. Nobody was killed and there was no serious trouble.

Around noon of the following day, Slade took a ride, following a trail that ran north by slightly west, over Hans Ragnal's Slash H range. He wanted a look at the mountains farther north, having a notion concerning those mountains.

He had covered several miles when he saw four horsemen riding toward him. Foremost was a big rugged-looking individual with a craggy, bad-tempered face and truculent eyes. As Slade drew near, he abruptly reined his horse sideways to block the track.

"Hold it!" he shouted in a rumbling voice. "That's far enough!"

Slade sent Shadow forward a few more paces before he drew rein.

"Just what do you mean?" he asked, his voice deceptively mild.

"I mean," growled the big fellow, "that we don't want any blankety-blank-blank railroaders on this range. Oh, I saw you palavering with old Dunn." He added a remark or two not complimentary to Mr. Dunn's immediate ancestry.

"Get back the way you come!"

"Just what authority have you to block an open trail, in Texas?" Slade returned, his voice still musically mild. "I don't see any badge on your shirt front."

"I got all the authority I need right here," the other answered. His hand dropped to his holster.

Then he froze, grotesquely, as did his three companions. They were staring into two yawning black muzzles that apparently had come from nowhere. And back of those rock-steady muzzles were the eyes of El Halcon.

CHAPTER
SIX

Slade spoke, all the music gone from his voice, which was like to steel grinding on ice.

"Fellow," he said, "you haven't enough of that kind of authority to brace a snail on a slick log. Now suppose *you* get back the way you came, while you're able to."

The big fellow flushed scarlet with fury. He mouthed and muttered.

"If you didn't have those irons lined on us, I'd haul you off your horse and wipe the ground with you," he declared. "I — yowp!"

The last word was shot from him as the big Colts moved like the flicker of a falcon's wing.

However, they had just slid back into the holsters from which they came. Slade dismounted with lithe grace, his hands empty.

"Well, what are you waiting for?" he asked pointedly.

With a howl of rage the big fellow flopped from his saddle and rushed. He was met by a straight left that rocked him back on his heels. He recovered, rushed again, and caught a straight right that rocked him back still farther. Again he rushed.

Slade glided forward a pace, measuring his man with his eye. But his foot slipped on a slick rock and he reeled off balance.

With a yell of triumph, the other closed with him and threw his thick arms around his waist.

"Buck's got the underholt!" one of the cowboys whooped. "Buck's got him!"

However, Buck hadn't "got" him. As he strove mightily, in vain, to sweep the Ranger off his feet, Slade's locked hands cupped under his chin, forcing his head up and back. Back and back! The strain on Buck's cervical vertebrae was more than he could stand. He loosened his hold, staggered free.

And Slade hit him, square and true on the angle of the jaw, with all his muscular two hundred pounds back of the blow.

Buck shot through the air, thudded to the ground, and stayed there. Slade's eyes flickered to the three cowhands. One had dropped a surreptitious hand to his gun butt.

"Don't," Slade told him. "I have no desire to kill you, but I will kill you if you pull it. I thought it was a gentlemanly wring with no hard feelings. I *didn't* think some skunk would try to start fanging."

Under the searing contempt in the Ranger's voice, the cowboy reddened, dropped his eyes, fumbled with his hands. His two companions regarded him disapprovingly.

"Feller, I guess you're right," one said to Slade.

"You're blankety-blank-blank right he's right!" boomed from the ground. Buck was sitting up, rubbing his swelling jaw. He leaped to his feet and strode forward, a grin splitting his craggy features, one huge hairy paw extended.

"Put 'er there, feller!" he shouted. "Any man who can knock me off my pins is my *amigo*! My handle's Buck Hardy. Put 'er there!"

Slade "put 'er there" and they shook, smiling into each other's eyes.

"Now fork your cayuse and come along with us," Hardy said as he swung into the saddle. "You gotta come along to the Bull's mansh, it's only a coupla miles off. Don't say no. I wanta show the Boss what a real man looks like. Come along!"

Slade accepted the invitation, for he was glad of the opportunity to get a look at the cantankerous Hans Ragnal who was so set against the railroad, and of whom Sheriff Ord was suspicious.

It was but a short ride to the Slash H casa. As they drew near, Slade saw a bulky old gent with a leonine head of hair sitting on the veranda, his boots propped on the rail. Hardy let out one of his earth-shaking bellows,

"Break out the big kettle, Boss, we're bringin' you a railroader for dinner!"

The boots hit the floor with a thump. "What the blankety-blank blue blazes are you talking about?" their owner bawled back. "Gone plumb loco at last, eh? Well, I'm not surprised. Been expectin' it to happen any day. Who is that feller, and why are you bringing' him here?"

"Because he licked me!" Buck howled. "Nigh to busted my jaw. Ain't been hit so hard since I told my mom I was too big for her to wallop anymore and she showed me I wasn't — with a skillet!"

"He *licked* you!"

"That's right."

The oldster, who Slade rightly guessed was the redoubtable Hans Ragnal, turned to him.

"Okay, son," he said. "If you walloped the big horned toad, you're plumb welcome, no matter what you are or where you come from. Light off and come in for coffee and a snack. One of you loafers look after his cayuse."

"I'll do it," said Hardy, swinging from the saddle. "Golly! but he's a beauty! The sorta critter a feller like you'd be 'spected to fork."

He was introduced to Shadow, who appeared to take a liking to him at once, and led the big black to the barn. Slade followed Ragnal into the spacious living room, the furnishings of which bordered on luxurious. Ragnal waved him to a chair and shouted an order to the cook. Sitting down himself, he regarded El Halcon with his hot little blue eyes.

"Hardy said you're a railroader," he remarked interrogatively.

"I am, at present, Sheriff Ben Ord's special deputy," Slade corrected. "But I at times lend a hand to Mr. James G. Dunn, the General Manager of the C. and P. Railroad System and my friend."

"The blasted railroad shouldn't have come through here," old Hans growled.

"Why not?" Slade countered.

"Because the infernal engines scare the fat off the cows and set fire to the grass," Ragnal retorted.

"Both in the category of rank superstition," Slade said.

Old Hans swelled like a turkey cock, his face flushed. But something in the steady eyes hard on his averted what appeared to be an imminent explosion. He muttered and fumed, but went no further. Slade continued to regard him.

"Mr. Ragnal," he said abruptly, "have you a family?"

Old Hans hesitated, his glance wavered, wandered about the room, centered on a crayon portrait of a sweet-faced old lady.

"My wife passed on nigh onto twenty years ago," he replied. "I had a boy. It was for him I built this holding to what it is, hoping to pass it on to him when the 'call' came to me. But — he died."

"And now you have only material possessions left?"

"Guess that's so," Ragnal said heavily.

Slade's eyes were suddenly all kindness as they rested on the lonely old man.

"Mr. Ragnal," he said in his deep, rich voice, "Mr. Ragnal, many years ago there was a Man who lived for others, who died for others. He was gentle. His voice was soft. But He could be stern, did He deem sternness was in order. It was He who thundered from a mountain crest,

" 'It is easier for a camel to pass through the eye of a needle than for a rich man to enter the Kingdom of God!'

"Mr. Ragnal, that parable is ofttimes misunderstood, ofttimes misinterpreted, because of which its message is lost. Gates of Jerusalem were called 'eye of a needle' because they were so shaped. An unladen camel could pass through them without difficulty, but not a laden camel with its burden we would call pack sacks bulging out on either side. Its burden had to be removed, or lessened, before it could pass through. That is what Our Lord wished to convey. Not that there was anything wrong in a man prospering, acquiring wealth. But let that wealth become an obsession, all that he lived for, all that he had, he had failed in his life's mission. Only by changing, by showing more regard for others, could he hope to find the Keys of the Kingdom.

"Mr. Ragnal, you just said that you strove and labored to build your property into the fine and valuable holding that it is, so you could pass it on to your son. Didn't it ever occur to you that other men might have a similar hope, might be trying to build something to pass on to *their* sons? The coming of the railroad through this section will bring that opportunity to many. You said you have no family. Mr. Ragnal, you are a man of wealth and influence. Change your attitude toward your fellowmen, think not of what you have but what you can give, and I'll guarantee that soon you will have one of the largest 'families' in this section of Texas, and be just as solicitous of them and their welfare as if they were your own flesh and blood."

Again old Hans' glance wavered. Again it rested on the crayon portrait hanging on the opposite wall.

"Seems almost as if I hear *her* talking," he said. "She believed as you believe, spoke as you spoke. But I'm afraid I didn't heed."

His eyes swung back to the Ranger's face and abruptly a whimsical smile brightened his bad-tempered old face, marvelously changing its expression.

"Slade," he said, "so far as years go, you're a young man, but somehow I get the feeling you are a very old one, old enough to talk down to me. Do you always have this effect on folks? Do you always make them do what you want them to do?"

"Sometimes," Slade replied. "By showing them what they have really been wanting to do all along, only they wouldn't admit it to themselves."

"By gosh!" said Ragnal, "I believe you've hit the nail square on the head. Okay, you win! As soon as old man Dunn gets back, I'll drop in on him and maybe we can get together on some things."

"I am sure you will be able to," Slade said, with a smile.

"Here's my hand on it," replied Ragnal. They shook.

"Come and get it!" sounded from the kitchen.

"Snack's ready," said Ragnal, and led the way to the dining room.

The cook, a Mexican, bowed low to El Halcon, which old Hans did not fail to note.

Slade voiced a greeting in Spanish, which pleased him greatly. He bowed again, even lower.

The snack was bountiful and tasty and they lingered over it, discussing various range matters.

"Come again, son, and soon," Ragnal urged when Slade departed, with Buck Hardy bellowing a similar invitation.

As he headed for town through the golden glow of the twilight, Slade remarked to Shadow.

"Well, there goes my prime suspect, according to Sheriff Ord's way of looking at it. Now who we got? Of course, I haven't definitely made up my mind relative to Buck Hardy. He's hot-tempered, belligerent, opinionated, always welcoming a row. Seems to be all right, but I'll have to hold my judgment in abeyance until I know a little more about him."

Shadow's answering snort was derisive.

"Oh, I know you took to him," Slade said, "but you could be wrong."

This time Shadow did not deign to reply, snortingly or otherwise.

Back at the Slash H casa old Hans held converse with the cook.

"Manuel, you seem to know him," he said, apropos of Walt Slade. "Just what is he, anyhow?"

"*Patron*," Manuel replied, "he is El Halcon. A strange man. Where there is trouble, injustice, sorrow, he appears. When he departs, he leaves behind him freedom from care, justice, gladness. There are those who say, reverently, that he is *One* returned to earth to right its wrongs. As to that, *patron*, I know not. But I do know that although in the hour of his wrath he is terrible, he is good."

"Manuel," old Hans replied slowly, "I think you have the right notion."

Just before he and Slade had parted, Ragnal said, "I'll have a talk with some of the other owners. I've a notion they'll follow my lead."

Slade thought that very likely they would. Little doubt but that Hans Ragnal had dominated the section for quite some time.

So as he rode to Redmon, he felt the day had been far from wasted. By giving Buck Hardy a going over he had won the respect of the Slash H outfit; and he had won old Hans over to his way of thinking, which might well prevent serious trouble between the railroad and the cattlemen of the section. Yes, he had made a start.

His main problem, of course, still confronted him. That somebody was endeavoring to hamper the railroad construction — more likely a number of somebodies — was plainly apparent. And, which was more seriously important from a Ranger's viewpoint, to the accompaniment of robbery and murder.

Was the M. K. crowd, Jaggers Dunn's rivals, back of the movement to slow up the C. & P. project? Not beyond the realm of possibility. Quite probably, in fact. But if so, Slade was of the opinion that the scalawags they sent in to do the chore had gotten completely out of hand and were going it on their own. Well, it wouldn't be the first time such a thing had happened, as certain prominent cattlemen who had brought in professional gunslingers to do their fighting for them had learned to their cost. Slade rode on through the deepening dusk, pondering the various angles of the problem and arriving at no satisfying conclusion.

When he reached Redmon, he briefly recounted the day's incidents for Sheriff Ord's edification. The old peace officer shook his grizzled head resignedly.

"How do you do it?" he marveled. "How *do* you do it! I wouldn't have believed there was a man living who could cause ornery old Hans Ragnal to do an about-face. And you took Buck Hardy down a peg, too? He's had it coming for a long time. Sets up to be the best man in the whole section, in all Texas, to hear him tell it. Guess he's changed his mind a mite.

"So I reckon we have to write Ragnal off the list, eh?"

"Looks a little that way," Slade replied. "I don't believe he has had anything to do with the things that have happened."

"How about Hardy?"

"I rather think him also, but frankly I'm not altogether sure about Hardy," Slade admitted. "He may be all right, and I repeat, I rather think so, but I'm not sure. He's an uncertain quantity. I really can't see him going in for robbery and murder, but acts against the railroad are a different matter. Knowing his boss was dead-set against the coming of the line, he might have thought it the smart thing to try and slow up operations. There is one thing, however, that makes me inclined to exonerate Hardy."

"What's that?" Ord wanted to know.

"That he lacks the technical knowledge displayed in the depredations against the line. That lets Hardy out, I fear."

"Then where the devil do we stand?" Ord growled.

"Right where we were; a little back of where we were, in fact, with the elimination of Hans Ragnal as a suspect. Have to start all over."

The sheriff swore dismally. "I'm hungry," he concluded. "Let's amble over to the Crow Bait for a bite. Maybe we can learn something there that'll help."

"I had a rather hefty snack with Ragnal, but I expect I can handle a sandwich and some coffee," Slade replied.

"And, as you said, it's just possible there might be a pleasant surprise in store for us."

For El Halcon there would be; definitely so.

CHAPTER
SEVEN

Although it was still quite early, the Crow Bait was already crowded when they arrived. But Mack Ware had reserved their favorite table, close to the dance floor, for them. They sat down and gave their order.

"Here come the gals," the sheriff remarked. "Now business will pick up."

Slade glanced absently toward the dance floor, for his thoughts were elsewhere.

The girls, in their short, spangled skirts and low-cut bodices, were indeed filing in from the dressing room.

Abruptly Slade stiffened in his chair.

"Well, I'll be hanged!" he exploded.

"Hope so," the sheriff said cheerfully, "but why?"

Slade did not answer, for he was still staring at the advancing group.

Leading the procession was a slender, graceful little thing with great sloe eyes, a creamily tanned complexion, and sweetly formed lips that were the scarlet of the hibiscus bloom. She had curly dark hair, and plenty of it, that glinted flashes of red in the lamp light. She glanced around the room and came prancing to the table.

"Marie Telo!" was his second explosion. "Where in blazes did *you* come from?"

"Laredo," she replied laconically, her great dark eyes dancing. "What's the matter, dear, can't a girl have itchy feet, too, and like to move around? I heard this was an interesting town, so I caught a train. There was a nice man with a buckboard when the train pulled in and he offered to drive me here, and that nice Mr. Ware gave me a job of dancing. That's what I am, you know, a dance floor girl."

"Did you know I was here?" he demanded.

"Remember, the Telos are also psychic and have the second sight, just as your Scotch ancestors," she replied. "So I guessed it."

"Yes, you guessed it, with the help of those grinning apes over on the platform," he retorted, shooting a glare at the musicians.

"Well, they did send me a telegram saying they thought I'd like it here," she admitted demurely. "Aren't you glad to see me?"

"Of course I'm glad to see you, but you'll be the death of me yet, with the capers you pull," he replied. "Like wading the Rio Grande by way of the Indian Crossing, with the whirlpools threatening any minute to sweep you off and smash you to pulp on the rocks. And like blowing an owlhoot from under his hat."

"He would have killed you if I hadn't," she replied soberly.

"You're right there," Slade agreed. He cast another glance toward the chortling musicians.

"So that's why those hellions had their heads together the other night," he said. "And Ware played right along with them."

"And wasn't he nice to give me a job and — a room upstairs?" Marie said innnocently. Sheriff Ord, who had been an interested listener, shook with laughter.

Slade pulled out a chair. "Sit down and have some wine," he told her. "How's Rosa, your sister, and her husband, Estaban?"

"They're fine," she answered. "They sent regards."

Sheriff Ord was introduced.

"Remember, you said we might get a pleasant surprise here tonight," he reminded El Halcon. "Looks like it worked out."

"Well, I couldn't have gotten a nicer one," Slade admitted, and was rewarded with a smile that flashed her little teeth against the scarlet of her lips, white and even as Slade's own.

"Of course I took a chance, showing up here unannounced," she said with a giggle. "For all I knew you might have been tied up with some of your other women; perhaps you are."

"Other women!" repeated Sheriff Ord, the most loyal of friends. "Betcha he hasn't got any. Why, he don't even look at the dance floor girls."

"Heavens! How he must have changed!" Marie exclaimed, with another giggle. "Soon as I finish my wine, I'll have to go back on the floor. Got to earn my keep!"

"Earn your keep!" Slade retorted. "Lots of need you have to earn keep. You're a rich woman, and you know it."

"Perhaps, in material things," she conceded, her beautiful eyes abruptly somber. "Oh, well, one of your favorite quotes — 'Gather ye rosebuds while ye may!'"

A moment later, she skipped back to the floor, her spangled skirt flaring, the sway of her hips expressive, to put it mildly.

"She's sure some looker," the sheriff said admiringly. "And 'pears to be as nice as she's pretty."

"She is," Slade stated, with emphasis. "But there was something to what she said, that a girl gets itchy feet, too, and wants to move around. This blasted pueblo will just suit her. She thrives on excitement, and danger. But a girl to ride the river with."

The sheriff nodded emphatic agreement to the highest compliment the rangeland can pay.

"She's pure Spanish blood and Texas born, as were her father and grandfather before her," Slade resumed. "And she's a true daughter of that great and illustrious Spanish family, the Telos, who did much in their days to keep the Spanish King on his throne. But the itchy feet were there even then, and her forbears, in steel and velvet, emigrated to the New World many, many years ago. Marie's father owned a good spread down around Laredo, but some scoundrels who called themselves the Land Committee murdered him — shoved him off a cliff — and got control of his holding. Marie went to work dancing in a cantina, a nice place, run by one Miguel Sandoval.

"However, her land was gotten back, and Marie and Rosa, her sister, sold a slice of their bottom lands holding to the irrigation project under way there for a

64

whopping big price. So Marie and Rosa and Rosa's husband, Estaban, are well heeled."

Slade failed to mention that he was responsible for the girls recovering their holding and the culprits being brought to justice, which shrewd old Sheriff Ord sensed.

"But Marie couldn't sit around doing nothing and went back to work, dancing in Miguel's cantina," Slade continued, "and moving around a bit. So it isn't so surprising that she should show up here."

"Not at all," the sheriff agreed dryly.

Mack Ware, the owner, strolled over to join them, his eyes twinkling.

"So you were a part of the conspiracy, too, Slade observed.

"Well," said Ware, "the orchestra boys told me they knew a nice girl down at Laredo who could pull good customers in with her dancing. I've always got an eye open for business, you know, so I sent her a wire offering her work here."

"And had a buckboard meet her at the train?"

"Well," repeated Ware, "I could hardly let her walk the forty miles or so. Her feet would have been sore and she wouldn't have been able to dance; just plain business."

"And you are an abominable liar," Slade said. But thanks for doing me a nice favor."

Ware chuckled, and motioned to a waiter, who at once headed for the bar.

"Let us drink," said Mr. Ware.

After emptying his glass, Ware returned to the end of the bar. The sheriff had wandered to a table across the room and was conversing with some acquaintances. Marie was on the floor.

So Slade, left alone, tried to relax with his smoke and his coffee, without much success. Not only was he weary of the constant din, but he was experiencing an uneasy premonition that all was not as it should be. He tried to combat it, but it refused to be downed, intensified, became more urgent.

Finally he gave up. He caught Marie's eye, waved his hand and sauntered out, the girl's gaze following him anxiously.

Outside, he wormed his way through the throng packing the sidewalks and after a bit reached Shadow's stable. Quietly, so as not to awaken the keeper if he happened to be asleep upstairs, he got the rig on the big black, led him out and mounted.

"Well, horse, we're going to play another loco hunch," he said. "Maybe nothing to it, but then again, considering the things that have happened lately, there might be a good deal. Anyhow, we'll go see. Nice to be out in the air, after all that smoke and hullabaloo. So let's go!"

Shadow, who didn't like being cooped up, snorted gaily and lengthened his stride. Overhead the stars were glowing silver that cast a soft sheen over the rangeland. The mountains to the west stood out stark and grim, and toward those glowering mountains, Slade turned his mount's head.

His objective was the cutting, which was deserted at this hour, with only a flicker of light here and there.

As he neared the scene of operations, Slade searched the terrain with eyes that missed nothing. All appeared peaceful enough, with no cause for alarm. But the hunch persisted, and in consequence his vigilance increased.

At the beginning of the cut he drew rein. Nearby was a clump of thicket. He hesitated a moment, then eased Shadow into the growth, dropped the split reins to the ground and dismounted.

"Got a notion I'll do better on my feet," he told the horse, in low tones. "You loom up like a mountain side, and your clumsy hoofs make a racket."

Shadow did not deign to reply to the obvious slander. Slade stroked his neck and glided toward the cut, keeping in the shadow as much as possible. He hadn't the slightest notion what he was looking for, but somehow felt it behooved him to be cautious.

Not far off, now, were several spur tracks that accommodated the locomotives and cars of materials. And close to one of the spurs was the flimsy wooden barracks in which most of the workers slept. Very likely there was nobody around but the engine watchman, whose duty was to see that the fires were properly banked, and that there was plenty of water in the boilers.

A sound smote Slade's ears — a common enough sound around railroad yards — the muffled boom of a safety valve. Nothing so strange about that, except that the sound persisted unduly. And threading through the low roar of the escaping steam was another sound, the purr of a blower going full blast. What the devil was the engine watchman trying to do, just waste coal? That racket cut loose by the safety valve indicated a boiler at full pressure, which was certainly not needed at this time of night.

His curiosity aroused, El Halcon glided toward the locomotive that was kicking up the racket, which sat on a spur almost against the barracks wall. He had nearly reached the steps that led to the cab when he halted to stand motionless, peering at what appeared to be the body of a man dressed in jumper and overalls.

It was a body, all right, no longer a man, for between the shoulder blades protruded the haft of a heavy knife.

And El Halcon understood!

He bounded forward, up the steps and into the cab. A glance at the steam gauge showed the pressure well above the maximum, despite the clamor of the wide-open safety valve. The water glass showed empty.

Slade flung open the fire door. In the furnace, fanned by the blower, was a raging fire. He seized the grate shaker, slid it into place and frantically worked the lever back and forth, dumping the fire on the ground beneath the engine.

Clouds of smoke and ash billowed up, filling the cab with murk and choking fumes.

From the darkness beyond the tracks to the right, a gun cracked. A bullet slammed against the side of the boiler. Another followed it, and still another, which barely grazed Slade's left hand.

Calmly, as if death were not spitting at him from the darkness and roaring at him from the burned belly of the locomotive, he worked the lever back and forth a couple more times before slamming the fire door shut, diving through the smoke that had doubtless saved him from stopping lead, and leaping out the far side of the gangway and to the ground. He landed on the balls of his feet, reeled, staggered, rocked back on his heels and caught his balance. Whirling, he whisked to the rear of the tender and around it.

Three men, guns in hand, were running toward the locomotive. Both Slade's Colts let go with a rattling crash. Answering slugs stormed about him. One ripped through his shirt sleeve. Another sliced the crown of his hat. He fired again and again as fast as he could squeeze the trigger.

Abruptly he realized no more lead was coming his way. Lowering his smoking guns, he gazed at the three forms sprawled motionless on the ground. He glided forward a couple of steps, guns ready for instant action. Having made sure there was nothing more to be feared from the trio, he began mechanically reloading.

Inside the barracks sounded shouts and curses. The door banged open and out streamed men in all stages of undress. Suddenly one voice rose above all others.

"Mr. Slade!" it boomed. Flaherty, the big foreman, came plowing to the front, shoving other men out of his way.

"What happened, Mr. Slade?" he bellowed. "What's going on?"

69

Slade nodded toward the locomotive, which was now perfectly quiet save for the lessening purr of the blower.

"Another three minutes, and that boiler would have exploded," he replied. "I'd say it would have blown out the whole side of the barracks and very likely killed anybody who happened to be bunking against that wall."

"Hell and blazes!" gasped Flaherty, "*I* was sleeping against that wall! Where's that blankety-blank engine watchman?"

"I think you'll find what's left of him just beyond the gangway steps," Slade replied.

Flaherty hurried in the direction indicated, squatted down and peered close.

"Yes," he said, straightening up, his voice abruptly quiet, "yes, it's him, poor Roony, the engine watchman. Murdered, wasn't he?"

"He was," Slade answered. Flaherty swore bitterly.

"Did you get any of his killers, Mr. Slade?" he asked hopefully.

Slade gestured with the muzzle of his Colt before sheathing it.

"Three on the ground over there," he replied. "I doubt if there were any more about."

Flaherty, others crowding after him, strode to take a look. He swore again, but this time exultantly.

"Fine! Fine!" he said. "Guess the sidewinders are beginning to know what it means to go up against El Halcon."

"El Halcon!" The name ran through the crowd. Men stared, almost in awe, at the man whose exploits were

70

fast becoming a legend throughout the Southwest, all over Texas and beyond, in fact.

"Sure fine that you happened along when you did, Mr. Slade," Flaherty said. "A notion you saved our bacon for quite a few of us."

"It is possible," Slade admitted. "Of course they might just have had slowing up the project in mind, but it wouldn't have troubled them had they killed several people, just as they did the engine watchman. It's a killer bunch.

"Yes, quite a scheme," he added. " 'Killed the watchman to get him out of the way, built up a big fire in the firebox and opened the blower to keep the draft going. As the water in the boiler lowered, the pressure built up despite the effort of the safety valve to relieve it. A little more and the crown sheet would have been burned and the pressure too great for the boiler to withstand. And away she would have gone."

"And away some of us would have gone," a listener put in. "Three cheers for Mr. Slade!"

The cheers were given, with a will. Slade smiled and bowed acknowledgment.

"Leave everything just as it is for the sheriff to see," he told them. "Flaherty, don't let anybody touch the bodies. Yes, leave the night watchman where he is till the sheriff gets a look at him. I'll see you all tomorrow. Now you'd better get back to bed and knock off a little shut-eye. Busy day tomorrow."

With a nod, and another smile, he walked to where Shadow waited, forked the saddle and headed for town.

"And, fellers," Flaherty said to the gathering, "there goes the Big Boss of this working. Mr. Thomas told me that Mr. Dunn has put him in charge, and whatever he says goes. I rec'lect him from another working, and my advice is, don't arg'fy with him if you hanker to stay healthy."

"Who'd want to!" replied a voice. "It'll be plumb fine to have him for the Old Man."

Walt Slade would have been pleased by that compliment. "Old Man" has nothing to do with age. It is the accolade of labor. Only a boss who is liked, respected, and admired can hope to have that title bestowed upon him by such workers as those hardy railroaders. To them, Slade would henceforth be the Old Man.

CHAPTER
EIGHT

Reaching the Crow Bait, Slade left Shadow standing at the rack. When he entered, Sheriff Ord shot him one glance and said,

"All right, let's have it. I know that look; you've been into something."

Slade told him, tersely. The sheriff had quite a few things to say. Fortunately, Marie was not at the table at the moment, for none of them were fit for a lady's ears.

"So I guess you'd better saddle your nag and ride over there with me for a look-see," Slade said. "Wait till I tell Marie everything is under control and we'll be back before long. Otherwise she'll be developing a case of the jitters."

"Boone is at the office, so I reckon I'd better tell him to tie onto a wagon and follow us, so we can pack the carcasses to town," the sheriff said. "Juan, the stable keeper, has one he'll let us have. Go ahead and talk to your gal; I'll meet you at the stable."

Marie was relieved. "But I'm not overly hopeful," she said, after Slade had explained matters. "You can't walk out the door without getting mixed up in something. That's always been the way, and you'll never change. I doubt you'll find me here on the floor when you get back. I'm tired and I'm going to quit early tonight. Mr. Ware said it would be okay. Be — seeing — you!" She smiled, and lowered her lashes.

"Guess Thomas and Graham must be in town, seeing as they didn't show up after the ruckus," the sheriff remarked as they got under way. "They sleep here, not at the barracks."

"Anyhow, they didn't put in an appearance," Slade replied.

"They'll put in one tomorrow, after they hear about what happened," Ord chuckled. "I'm of a notion they're going to be plumb flabbergasted."

With Flaherty standing guard, the bodies were right where Slade left them. They were examined by the light of a lantern. Their pockets revealed nothing of importance, save considerable money, which the sheriff took charge of.

But once again, the overall pocket seams of one interested Slade, although he did not comment.

Less than an hour later, Deputy Boone arrived with the wagon. The bodies were loaded, including that of the murdered engine watchman.

"Just wait till we hit town with this load," Ord chuckled. "There's going to be a real hullabaloo."

The sheriff proved to be no mean prophet. There was excitement aplenty when the wagon trundled through the streets with its grisly cargo. Soon the sheriff's office was crowded with people exclaiming, asking questions.

74

Ord took it on himself to do the explaining. Admiring glances were cast at Slade. A number insisted on shaking hands and congratulating him.

With the rumpus at its height, Doctor Sam Clay strolled in, eyed the bodies a moment and chuckled.

"Think I'll move my residence to here," he said, "now that El Halcon, the notorious owlhoot, has squatted here there'll be plenty of business for me, as coroner. Not as a doctor; when he gets through with 'em, a doctor ain't needed. Has anybody got the undertaking concession? He's the jigger who's going to get rich."

The crowd laughed at his banter. This time several persons were positive they had seen one or more of the outlaws in town but were vague as to just when and where and under what conditions.

"That's the trouble with cowhands," somebody remarked. "They all dress alike, all look alike, so you can hardly tell one from another, and you don't pay much attention to 'em. I'm sure I saw that chunky one hanging around some rumhole, but just which one I ain't sure."

Which was the general reaction and didn't surprise Slade but caused the sheriff to indulge in some profanity.

"You figure there's some hellion, a smart one, running the pack?" he asked in low tones of El Halcon.

"Well," the Ranger replied, "I've never yet seen anything all tail and no head, and that goes for owlhoots, too. Yes, I'm sure there's somebody running the show, planning the moves and instructing the hired hands how to put them into execution. Who? That's your question, and at the moment I'd say your guess is as good as mine."

"I doubt it," growled Ord. "I've a notion right now you've got your eye on some wind spider."

Slade smiled, but did not otherwise comment.

"I'll hold an inquest around noon so we can get rid of these cadavers and make room for the next batch," Doctor Clay said. "That all right with you, Walt?"

"That'll be fine," Slade agreed. "And now I'm going to call it a night; been a busy day."

"Good hunting," said the sheriff.

Old Doc was good as his word and the inquest was held shortly after noon. "The unfortunate engine watchman met his death at the hands of parties unknown, presumably the three sidewinders who got just what was coming to them," said the verdict.

Morris Thomas, the construction engineer, was present at the inquest and after the bodies were removed he talked with Slade, lauding him for his exploit of the night before.

"I'm confident you saved lives, Mr. Slade," he said. "Without a doubt that flimsy old shack would have collapsed completely when one side was blown out. Yes, it was a wonderful piece of work.

"I sent Graham right back to the project before I came here," he added. "Wanted somebody with authority in charge. Incidentally he feels very bad about that mistake we made. Blames himself, seeing as he did

76

the calculating. But I ran the lines and should have caught it, so I feel I am equally to blame."

"Everybody makes mistakes," Slade replied. "We'll soon have it straightened out."

"Graham is a good man," the engineer continued. "He came highly recommended and I hired him. Mr. Dunn okayed it without question."

"As I said, Mr. Dunn has confidence in you," Slade replied noncommitally.

"Well, I'm heading for the cutting," Thomas said. "Will I see you there later?"

"Yes, I'll be there in a little while," Slade told him. "I desire to have a talk with the boys; may make some changes."

"Whatever you say goes, of course," Thomas answered, and took his departure.

"Seems to be all right," Sheriff Ord commented.

"Yes, he seems so," Slade agreed. Ord shot him a glance, but asked no questions.

A little later, Slade did ride to the cutting. He dismounted and walked about, studying the operation. Finally he beckoned Flaherty, the foreman.

"Terence," he said, "there are too many men trying to work in this cramped cutting, and the tunnel will be even worse. They are getting in each other's way and slowing up the work in consequence. I'm going to start a night shift."

"By gosh! Mr. Slade, that's a notion," the foreman instantly agreed. "I'm willing to bet it'll pay off."

"That's the way I feel about it," Slade said. "I'll leave picking the men for the shift to you. And here's another chore for you: I want you to select three men of good courage and who can shoot. Arm them and have them patrol the workings at night."

"That's a notion, too," said Flaherty. "May put a stop to the shenanigans that have been going on here."

"Now call the boys together," Slade directed. "I wish to talk to them."

Flaherty did so, and quickly an expectant crowd gathered. Briefly, Slade outlined his plan for a night shift.

"And something else," he added. "You know what footage you are supposed to gain each day. From now on, there'll be a bonus for every additional foot above the quota."

There was a moment of silence; then a voice boomed.

"Hurrah for the Old Man!"

Slade smiled, greatly pleased, and waved his hand in acknowledgment.

"You've got 'em, Mr. Slade, every ornery spalpeen of 'em," chuckled Flaherty. "From now on they'll follow you to hell and back if you say the word. Yep, they're yours! Anything else?"

"Not for the present," Slade replied. "I'm going to the office to inform Mr. Thomas of the change."

Slade found Thomas and Graham both in the office. He outlined briefly the changes he had made while the engineers listened attentively.

"You are right, Mr. Slade," Thomas said. "We will undoubtedly get better results working two shifts."

Graham nodded agreement.

78

"That's the great advantage of having absolute authority," Thomas continued. "Without it, one hesitates to make drastic changes without first consulting higher authority. Sometimes even hesitates to broach them."

Graham nodded again, a speculative look in his light eyes as they rested on the Ranger. He spoke for the first time, asking a question.

"Do you contemplate making other changes, Mr. Slade?"

"Only if conditions cause me to consider it expedient to do so," Slade replied. "For the present, no."

Satisfied that everything was under control, for the time being at least, Slade returned to Redmon and a confab with Sheriff Ord. He found the old law enforcement officer alone, smoking his pipe and contemplating the floor, which was now devoid of bodies.

"Those hellions," he remarked, "looked like cowhands, all right, didn't you think?"

"They never were," Slade replied. "No marks of rope or branding iron on their hands. I would say, however, that at some time they were employed at construction work." He was silent for a few moments, his eyes thoughtful, while the sheriff waited expectantly. Abruptly he remarked,

"The type of overalls favored by cowhands and those worn by the construction workers are much the same."

"They are," agreed Ord. "What of it?"

"Nothing except something peculiar about those worn by one of the pair who tried to drygulch us in the Comstock and by one of the three handling the chore of blowing up the locomotive."

"Yes?" the sheriff prompted.

"Yes," Slade repeated. "In both instances there was a caking of rock dust in the pocket seams."

"Meaning the devils had been hanging around the cutting?" Ord at once guessed.

"Exactly," Slade said. "I think they had been working there. And there was something else I noticed. Both had recently shaved, but the texture and coloring of the skin of chin and cheeks showed that they had not previously shaved for some days."

"And what about that?"

"A straggle of beard will greatly change a man's appearance," Slade explained. "Quills inserted in his nostrils, and a little putty properly applied will give him a different shaped nose. A couple of blackened teeth would also help."

"Meaning that without the whiskers and the other stuff, the fellers they worked alongside of wouldn't recognize them?"

"That's just what I mean," the Ranger conceded.

"And you figured it all out because there was rock dust in their pockets and they'd just recently shaved! Is there anything you don't notice?" sighed the sheriff.

"It is hard to overlook things that are so obvious," Slade replied smilingly.

"Well, I overlooked 'em, and so did everybody else," countered Ord. "Why were the devils working in the cutting? Looked to me like the sort that wouldn't work at anything if they could help it."

"In a way they couldn't help it, if they wished to put over the chore that had been handed them and for

80

which they were being paid," Slade answered. "They were working at the cutting to get the low-down on things, which would enable them to put into effect the schemes planned by whoever is the head of the pack and does the thinking."

"Guess you're right on all counts," the sheriff admitted.

"Without a doubt," Slade continued, "it is a well organized and close-knit outfit that is endeavoring to slow up progress for the railroad, and, in the meanwhile, branching out on their own with such nice matters as robbery and murder in mind. Which is of interest to us as law enforcement officers."

"You're darn right," growled Ord. "And you figure the head man of the bunch has lost control?"

"No, I do not," Slade differed. "It is the outfit which hired him to make trouble for the C. and P. that has lost control. Their big mistake was putting him on their payroll, which they may learn to their cost. I am of the opinion that he not only condones the acts of his followers but is hand-in-glove with them, profiting as they profit. Usually the way with that sort. He'll try to deliver the goods where the railroad is concerned, so long as he thinks it is to his advantage to do so, but quick and easy money is his paramount objective. Plus, perhaps, the gratification of a blood lust as an added incentive."

"And what the heck are we going to do about it?" demanded the sheriff.

"First find out for sure who he is, then drop a loop on him," Slade replied.

"Which figures to be something of a chore," Ord growled.

"No doubt," Slade agreed carelessly. "However, we have handled such chores before and I expect we'll make out."

"Yes, the chances are we will," Ord admitted, "but I've a notion we're in for a few headaches before the last brand is run. How about something to eat?"

Slade was agreeable to the suggestion and they repaired to the Crow Bait Corral to satisfy that want.

It was well past sunset and the dusk was deepening. Before entering the saloon, they paused to gaze westward. Under the gloom of the mountain, lights were twinkling. Evidently Flaherty had gotten his night shift going without delay.

"A good man, who's due for a nice boost in salary," Slade commented, referring to the big foreman.

"Do you think Thomas is put out by you taking over?" Ord asked as they sat down and gave their order.

"Doesn't seem to be," Slade answered. "Wouldn't be surprised if he feels relieved. Now if a mistake is made, he won't have to shoulder the blame."

"You ain't very good at making mistakes, so I expect there won't be any to shoulder," the sheriff said.

"Hope you're right," Slade smiled. "But it's a tricky business and any slip can cause trouble."

"Here come the dancers," Ord remarked, "and your slip of a gal is heading this way to tell you to give account of yourself.

"Honey, you sure look fine," he added as Marie plumped into a chair beside him. "Eyes all bright and

82

shiny and your cheeks plumb full of roses. You must have had a real good night's sleep."

Under the twinkle in his eyes, Marie blushed.

She had a glass of wine with them and then trotted to the floor, for business was picking up and the girls were in demand.

After he finished eating, the sheriff joined some acquaintances at the bar for a confab. Slade sat smoking, and pondering recent events.

All in all, he felt he was not doing too badly. Five of the devils accounted for and a catastrophe averted that might well have meant mass murder. Nor did he discount inducing a change of heart on the part of old Hans Ragnal, which might also prevent a killing or two should a real row develop between the ranchers and their hands and the railroaders. That situation was packed with dynamite and it wouldn't take much to touch off an explosion.

However, he did not underestimate the task that confronted him. Without doubt he had arrayed against him a shrewd and ruthless individual who would stop at nothing to achieve his ends. Well, he had gone up against such before and had always managed to make out, so why worry. He ordered more coffee and relaxed comfortably.

CHAPTER
NINE

Now the boom town was, as usual, at the peak of its noisy rampage, and the Crow Bait seemed to be the focus of activity. The bar was lined two deep, every table occupied. The two roulette wheels were spinning gaily, the faro bank was busy, the dance floor was so crowded the dancers could do little more than shuffle, to which nobody showed signs of objecting; it just meant closer embrace.

Slade remained where he was, studying the crowd, for he had concluded that sooner or later everybody in Redmon showed up at the Crow Bait.

So he was not particularly surprised when Morris Thomas, the engineer, walked in, found a place at the bar and ordered a drink. He evidently had not noticed El Halcon, and Slade did not announce his presence. However, he regarded Thomas with interest.

Abruptly he realized he was not the only one present who showed an interest in the engineer. Two men in rangeland clothes standing a little farther down the bar were also giving him attention. Their hat brims were drawn low, their faces in the shadow, but El Halcon's keen vision noted the sideways glint of their eyes focusing on the railroader. Their heads drew together;

84

evidently they were speaking to each other in very low tones, for Slade could only catch the indistinguishable mutter of their voices amid the din. He divided his attention between them and Thomas. They seemed to say a few more words, shoved their glasses aside and walked out. Slade again caught that sideways glint of eyes.

Thomas turned from the bar and surveyed the room. His gaze centered on Slade and he waved his hand. The Ranger gestured to the vacant chair opposite him. Thomas nodded his understanding, sauntered across to the table and sat down. Slade beckoned a waiter to bring drinks.

"Just loafing around a bit and relaxing before going to bed," Thomas said. "I have a little shack over on Park Avenue. Isn't much to look at, but it's comfortable. Less noise and confusion than the barracks. Graham lives on Grand Avenue. Things are sure lively here. Somehow, though, I like it. I've been at camps before, but never anything that quite equalled this. She's a humdinger."

"Yes, she's that, all right," Slade agreed. "Here comes Sheriff Ord."

"Yep, and here comes your gal," Ord said as he sat down and beckoned a waiter. "Guess she figures she has to keep an eye on you; good judgment."

Thomas was introduced to Marie who joined them in a glass of wine before returning to the floor.

"Darling, I just love this place," she said to Slade. "Always something going on. Maybe we'll have a nice fight later. Only don't you get mixed up in it. Let them pummel one another, good for them. And as you once told me, nobody should interfere in a private fight, not good manners."

Thomas laughed heartily and regarded her with admiration. Marie crinkled her eyes at him, slanted a glance at Slade.

"Someday you'll stop a thrown bottle with your classic nose, and then it won't be classic anymore," he predicted.

"Might be an improvement," she returned blithely. "I've always thought a retroussé nose cute." Thomas laughed again.

Marie finished her wine and scampered back to the floor. Ord tossed off his snort, ordered another drink all around and moved to the bar for a few minutes. Thomas emptied his glass and glanced at the clock.

"Really I'll have to be going," he said. "Want to be on the job early. Any orders for tomorrow, Mr. Slade?"

"Yes," the Ranger replied. "Haul out your transit and check the cutting grade. I don't think Flaherty will make a slip, but it's best not to take chances on a mistake that would require work being done over."

"You're right," Thomas agreed soberly. "After the one I made, I'm on the lookout for everything. One such is enough and more than enough; we can do without a repeat. See you tomorrow, then."

With a smile and a nod he departed. Slade watched him through the swinging doors; then, obeying a sudden impulse, stood up and followed.

Outside he had no difficulty spotting his man, who was sauntering along leisurely. Slade kept a score or so paces back, confident that in the poor lighting, Thomas wouldn't recognize him if he happened to look around, which he didn't. When he did turn, it was into Park Avenue. Slade quickened his gait and when, in turn, he rounded the corner, he was not more than a dozen paces behind the engineer, who still sauntered along leisurely.

Now the Comstock saloon was only about thirty yards distant. And before the window two men were standing, their gaze fixed up the street. Slade instantly recognized them as the pair that had appeared to take an interest in Thomas in the Crow Bait. Abruptly they started up the street. Another moment and they whisked into a dark alley mouth. The unconscious engineer kept on walking.

Slade bounded forward. Just as Thomas reached the edge of the alley, he seized him by the shoulder and hurled him back and off his feet as a gun blazed from the alley mouth; the bullet hissed past Slade's face.

From the alley sounded exclamations of anger. The two men bulged forth, shooting as they came. Which was a mistake on their part.

Weaving, ducking, slithering, Slade whipped out both guns and fired left and right, and again. A slug just touched his cheek. Another ripped through the shoulder of his shirt, drawing blood. He shot again with both hands.

One of the drygulchers crumpled up and fell like a sack of old clothes. The other half turned, as though to flee, then plunged forward on his face. Both lay without sound or motion.

Thomas had regained his feet, yammering, exclaiming in a dazed fashion.

"You all right?" Slade asked, without turning; he was taking no chances with one of the devils playing possum in hopes of getting the drop on him before passing out.

"Yes — yes," gasped Thomas. "I'm all right, thanks to you. What does it mean? Did they intend to kill me?"

"They did," Slade replied laconically as he lowered his guns and began reloading, being sure there was nothing more to fear from the pair on the ground.

"Good heavens! What *does* it mean?" said the engineer. "I didn't think I had an enemy in the world."

"Perhaps you haven't," Slade replied. "But perhaps you are in somebody's way and they decided to remove you. Such things have happened, you know." Thomas looked utterly bewildered.

Now men were streaming from the nearby Comstock, running up the street. Slade saw that most of them were railroaders. One shouted,

"Mr. Slade! It's Mr. Slade! What happened, Mr. Slade? What was all the shooting about?"

"I'll tell you what happened," Thomas shouted before Slade could reply. "He saved my life, at the risk of his own. That's what happened."

There was an instant of stunned silence. Then for the second time that day, a voice shouted,

"Hurrah for the Old Man!"

Brawny men crowded around Slade, to exclaim, swear, shake his hand and pat his back.

88

Finally, after considerable effort, he managed to halt the uproar and change the subject.

"Somebody hustle to the Crow Bait, please, and fetch Sheriff Ord," he directed. A man sped off to take care of the chore.

"And drag those bodies into the light and look them over," the Ranger added. "Perhaps somebody will recall seeing them before."

The bodies were hauled out, turned over on their backs. Men peered into the dead faces.

"Say!" exclaimed a big trackman, "I'll swear I've seen both these devils, working in the cut. Looked sorta different it seems to me, but I'll bet my last peso it was them. See the cross-shaped scar on this one's face? I remember noticing that scar and wondering how he come to get such a funny shaped one. Yep, I remember them both. Don't remember seeing them the last few days, though. Looks like maybe they had a grudge against Mr. Thomas for some reason or other. Did you bawl somebody out for something or other of late, Mr. Thomas, or maybe give them their walkin' papers?"

"Why — why really, with hundreds of men on the job, it is hard to say," the engineer replied. "I have to scold somebody now and then, but it's been quite a while since I discharged anybody. However, we'll have the bookkeeper check the payroll and see if anybody is missing."

Other men were confident they remembered the pair working in the cutting. However, Slade knew the power of suggestion is strong and people will be inclined to think what they wish to think. But the identification of the trackman, based on the oddly shaped scar, appeared fairly well-founded and corroborated his own opinion that members of the outlaw bunch had infiltrated the workers. "How many more of the devils?" he wondered.

The big trackman moved alongside El Halcon, lowered his voice.

"The boys won't forget this one, either, Mr. Slade," he said. "They like Mr. Thomas; he's a good man." He glanced around; lowered his voice still more.

"But just between you and me, he's a mite too easygoing to boss such a bunch of hellions as this. I talk nice to my boys so long as they'll let me, but I've found a pick handle is a darn good persuader if nice talkin' don't work."

Slade smiled. "You are a gang foreman?" he asked.

"That's right," the other replied. "Under Flaherty."

"What's your name?"

"Packy Maclain," the other answered. Slade nodded and put the name in the back of his mind for future reference.

"Here comes the sheriff!" somebody shouted.

Ord arrived, puffing, and demanded particulars. Thomas supplied them, so far as he knew.

"And if Mr. Slade hadn't happened to be walking behind me, I wouldn't be here telling about it," he concluded.

"Uh-huh, he has a habit of 'happening'," Ord said dryly. "Say, looks like everybody in town is here; word sure got around in a hurry. No wonder, though, that jigger you sent to tell me I was wanted busted in bellerin' like a steer with its tail caught in a barbed wire

90

fence. All right, some of you work dodgers pack the carcasses to my office and lay 'em on the floor. Deputy Boone will be there. Tell him I'll be along shortly."

Slade turned to Thomas, who still looked a bit white and shaken.

"You'd better get to bed," he advised. "Never mind about that transit work in the morning. You've had a harrowing experience. Try and sleep late."

"I'll be on the job," the elderly engineer declared sturdily. "Thank you again. Be seeing you."

"'Pears to be considerable of a feller," remarked Ord. He chuckled.

"Your little gal just shrugged her shoulders and threw out her hands," he said. "Guess she's used to it. How did you come to catch on what was in the makin'?"

Slade explained, in detail.

"I thought those two hard-looking characters were taking a mite too much interest in Thomas," he concluded. "So when he left I ambled along behind him, just in case."

"Darn lucky for him you did," growled Ord. "But why did they want to kill him?"

"Because, like myself, he's in somebody's way," Slade replied. "I'll have to keep an eye on him, although I doubt they'll try it again."

"Any notion who it is he's in the way of?" the sheriff asked.

"A question to which I'd very much like to have the for sure answer," Slade said.

"Just the same, I'm of the notion you do have a sorta notion," Ord said.

"Possibly, a sort of hazy notion, with nothing positive on which to base it. Just putting two and two together and making a little more than five, which is mathematically absurd," Slade smiled.

"Uh-huh, but you make figures stand up on their hind legs and paw the air," the sheriff declared. "Well, here we are, and looks like everybody else is here, too."

There was indeed a crowd of the curious in the office and it took the sheriff some time to shoo them all out. After which, with the door shut and locked, the bodies were carefully examined, with negative results, so far as Slade could see. The pockets discovered nothing of significance save considerable money, which the sheriff stowed away.

"How about the pocket seams, any more rock dust?" he asked.

"Freshly laundered overalls, no dust of any kind," Slade replied. "Doesn't matter. I'm convinced they worked in the cutting for a while. May be no more, but then again there could be. Wish I could catch one alive. Might be able to induce him to do a little talking."

"You shoot too darn straight for that," snorted Ord.

"Well, with the odds against me, I can hardly risk picking my targets," Slade replied smilingly. "Just have to aim for the thickest part and let it go at that."

"Well, guess there's nothing more to be done here," said Ord. "Just some more work for Doc Clay. Suppose we amble over to the Crow Bait for a snort or two and another bite to eat. All this excitement makes me hungry. And your little gal will be wondering if you've got mixed up in something else."

Slade was agreeable and they headed for the saloon.

When they arrived, Marie at once joined them and the story of what had happened was repeated for her benefit. She shook her curly head resignedly and let it go at that, except for glancing at the clock.

CHAPTER
TEN

Around mid morning, Slade rode to the cutting. He found Thomas in his office. He grinned, and handed Slade a sheet covered with figures. El Halcon studied them and nodded approval.

"Everything okay, just as I expected," the Ranger said.

"I checked and rechecked," Thomas remarked. "Flaherty is following directions. A good man."

"A very good man," Slade agreed. "I'm going out and have a talk with him."

"Go ahead," Thomas replied. "I have a few loose ends to tie up here. See you later."

Locating the foreman, Slade drew him aside.

"Terence," he said, "what is your opinion of Packy Maclain, one of your gang foremen?"

"Don't come any better," Flaherty instantly returned. "A hard worker, keeps his men in line, and knows his business."

"Then," Slade said, "I think I'll put him in charge of the night shift. You need an assistant you can depend on. As it is, you're working yourself to death trying to hold down two jobs. Oh, I heard about you being around at midnight when you should have been asleep."

"Well, I just figured I should keep an eye on things for a bit," the big foreman replied, apologetically. He chuckled.

"Seems to me you are on the job about twenty-four hours a day, from what I've heard," he added. "That was certainly fine, what you did for Mr. Thomas last night. Wish I'd been alongside you with a pick handle."

"Would have been a help," Slade conceded. "If you'd managed to whack one of the sidewinders with it, we might have been able to take him alive, which I would very much like to have done."

"You'll sink your hooks in one, sooner or later," the foreman said confidently. "There's that old loco over there that you kept from blowing up and salavating a bunch of us."

"The devils made a mistake, either through ignorance or lack of opportunity," Slade said. "If they'd screwed down the safety valve, she would have cut loose sooner, before I got here."

"I heard that darn valve bellerin'," Flaherty replied. "Wondered why it was keeping up so long. But I was half asleep and didn't pay it much mind. Didn't get up to see what was wrong with it."

"Very fortunate that you didn't," Slade answered. "I think that was why they were hanging around, to take care of anybody who might seek to interfere. Yes, quite likely you would have gotten yourself killed, like the poor devil of an engine watchman."

"Guess that's so," said Flaherty, drawing a deep breath. "Guess it was just my night for luck."

"Fetch Maclain," Slade directed. Flaherty hurried off to locate the gang foreman. Slade rolled a cigarette, leaned against Shadow's shoulder and waited.

After a bit, Flaherty returned with Maclain, who was greatly pleased by his unexpected promotion.

"I'm sure proud of your confidence in me, Mr. Slade," he said. "You can be plumb sure it won't be misplaced."

"Terence recommended you and I have faith in his judgment," El Halcon replied.

"Guess you don't need any recommendin' from anybody," Maclain chuckled. "Figure when you make up your mind, that's it."

"Now you'd better knock off for the rest of the day," Slade told him. "Go to town and have a few drinks and then try and get a little more sleep. Be seeing you both; I'm riding up to the head of the cut."

The two railroaders gazed after him, and in their faces was a brightness not of the sun.

"A real boss," Maclain remarked. "Thinks of his men first and all the time. Yes, the Old Man is a boss worth working for."

Slade rode slowly up the cut, which was now more than a mile in length. As he rode, he studied the sides, and arrived at a certain decision. When he reached the head, where the drills were driving into the granite, he drew rein and gazed up the long and very gentle slope to the notch.

"About three more days and we'll start driving the tunnel," he observed to Shadow. "Just about finished

96

with the granite rind, and from then on we'll be boring through broken shale. Will take considerable shoring but shouldn't present any real difficulty. That is, if the smart hellion doesn't figure some slick scheme to cause trouble. Well, we'll see. I've a notion he'll be somewhat circumspect from now on. However, that will make him all the more dangerous; whatever he evolves won't be obvious."

Turning the big black's head, he rode back down the cut, and again summoned Flaherty.

"Terence," he told the foreman, "when we start driving the tunnel, which will be day after tomorrow or the next day, you will have plenty of spare manpower. So I want you to start widening the cut, from beginning to end. I want it wide enough to accommodate three tracks instead of the two originally planned. A long siding here, and another in the cut at the far end of the tunnel will prevent tie-ups and delays and be real time savers once the trains start running."

"By gosh, you're right there," Flaherty instantly agreed. "That would have been my notion. Remember the trouble they had over at Plainton with tunnel delays, and a pile-up to boot when two of 'em got together in that hole, due to a dispatcher's slip? Sidings there would have saved that wreck."

Before returning to Redmon, Slade dropped in at the office to acquaint Thomas with his decision, as he felt courtesy required him to do. Graham, the mathematician, was also present. Both listened with absorbed interest as El Halcon outlined his plan.

"It will cost a lot of money," Graham remarked when the Ranger paused.

"Well, the C. and P. isn't exactly poverty stricken, and it will pay off in the end," Slade said. "There is going to be heavy traffic over this line once it reaches its western terminal."

"Anyhow, you're the boss, and what you say goes," Thomas said with a smile. "And I myself can see the advantages that will very likely accrue."

After Slade departed, the two engineers regarded each other.

"Well, what do you think?" Thomas asked.

"One thing is sure for certain," Graham replied. "Dunn has given him carte blanche and there's no arguing with him. The old man must be in his debt for help he's given at one time or another."

Graham's guess was a shrewd one; Jaggers Dunn was indebted to Slade for past assistance, including the saving of his life, which the Ranger had once done at the risk of his own.

"Well, we're doing all right with our railroad building," Slade observed to Shadow as they jogged along toward Redmon. "But when it comes to the chore we're really here to take care of, we're not making much progress. A few hired hands knocked off, but the head of the pack is very much on the loose and is no doubt right now plotting some deviltry. Okay, don't be fussing; things will work out, they always do."

Shadow, who was not fussing, tossed his head and snorted a derisive note.

When he reached the sheriff's office, Slade found Ord resting comfortably in his chair, his feet on the desk, contemplating the blanketed forms on the floor.

"Doc's holding an inquest in about an hour from now," he announced. "He sent word to Thomas to be here and Thomas said he would. Doc said again he's taking up permanent residence here for so long as you are around. To heck with the county seat! Nothing ever happens there."

"He'll be on the move to somewhere, soon, anyhow," Slade replied. "This makes a good stopping point for him, the kind of a pueblo he likes. A chuck line riding cowhand has nothing on him. Always got to be on the go. He'll never change." The sheriff chuckled, and twinkled his eyes at the Ranger.

"And I can see you at his age, maverickin' around from pillar to post. You won't change, either. Your gal hit the nail on the head when she said that."

"May fool you both," Slade said cheerfully. "Lots of time ahead of me.

"Or none at all," he added. "'The moving Finger writes . . .'"

The inquest was held as scheduled. Morris Thomas, a good talker, rendered a dramatic account of the killings, lauding Slade to the skies. The jury added its praise and returned a verdict of justifiable homicide on the part of a law enforcement officer. Which surprised no one.

Slade spent the rest of the afternoon strolling about the town. For Redmon was a town rather than a temporary construction camp such as would be erected on the far side of the mountains. Without a doubt, it was permanent, being strategically situated so far as trade was concerned.

El Halcon visited quite a few places, including the Comstock, where he was warmly greeted by Grimshaw, the owner.

"We've got the making of a good town, once the varmints are cleaned out, Mr. Slade," he said. "Betcha we end up getting the county seat. Sure hope you decide to coil your twine here; we can sure use you."

Slade thanked him, accepted a cup of coffee in lieu of a drink, and continued his stroll after giving the Comstock patrons a careful once-over. Aside from one or two individuals of doubtful status, he decided they weren't as bad as Sheriff Ord maintained. Mostly the younger cowhands and construction workers. Apt to kick up a ruckus now and then, but with no real harm in them.

He watched the sunset flame in splendor over the mountains, then made his way through the blue dusk to the Crow Bait Corral, where Marie Telo, with the sheriff to keep her company, was awaiting him.

"A whole day and you haven't been into something," she marveled. "Will wonders never cease!"

"Give him time, give him time," said the sheriff. "Day ain't over till midnight and that's quite a way off."

"I suppose you're right," she conceded. "Well, on to the floor; looks like it's going to be a busier night than usual. Just the same, I like it. Guess I'm naturally a hoyden at heart. Music and noise do things to me; I find them exhilarating, especially if — if — so long, be seeing you." She flounced off to the floor.

"Hello!" the sheriff exclaimed, "there's Neale Graham at the bar. He drops in here now and then, but spends most of his loafing time at the Comstock. Guess he's sorta like your gal, likes noise and excitement. Usually plenty of both in that blasted rumhole."

Slade had already noticed the mathematician standing at the bar, toying with a glass, an abstracted look on his ruggedly handsome face. After a little he turned; swept the room with his pale eyes. His gaze focused on Slade and the sheriff and he nodded cordially.

"Shall I call him over?" Ord asked as they returned the greeting.

"Not a bad idea," Slade replied. Ord beckoned.

The engineer responded, accepting a chair and the drink Slade ordered.

"How are you?" he asked. "Thought I'd loaf around a little and relax. Been a busy day."

For a while they indulged in light conversation. Graham's gaze wandered to the dance floor.

"See there's a new girl," he remarked, his eyes resting on Marie.

"The musicians knew her in Laredo and persuaded her to come here," Slade said quickly, before the sheriff could speak.

Graham's gaze lingered. "Sure nice looking," he remarked. "Wonder if she would dance with me?"

"Well, that's what she's on the floor for, to dance with the customers," Slade smiled. "Why not ask her?"

101

His eyes met Marie's for an instant and his head moved in an almost imperceptible nod; he knew well that Marie understood perfectly.

"I will ask her," Graham said. "I like her looks." He got up and moved to the edge of the dance floor as the number ceased. Marie managed to be close to where he stood. Graham spoke to her and she smiled acceptance. The music started and they fell into step.

Graham proved to be a good dancer. Slade could see her lips moving, and Graham's. The sheriff smothered a grin under his mustache.

"If you hanker to learn something about the gent, you'll learn it," he muttered. "The little gal's got him to talking, and I figure she's plumb smart and will lead him on just as she wants to. Expect he'll spill everything 'fore she's through with him."

"I am of the opinion that he will, definitely," Slade replied.

"I see now why you were so quick to tell him the orchestra boys brought her here," the sheriff added. "Didn't want him to know she's tied up with you, eh?"

"Exactly," Slade said. "Well, here comes our chuck and we might as well get busy on it."

CHAPTER
ELEVEN

Graham danced three numbers with Marie, then brought her to the table and bought a bottle of wine, as was the custom. She nodded casually to Slade and the sheriff and turned her attention to the engineer.

Finally Graham glanced at the clock. "I'll have to be going," he said. "But I'll come back tomorrow night or the next night."

"Please do," Marie said.

"I'll be sure to," he promised, said goodnight to Slade and the sheriff and departed. Slade regarded the girl expectantly.

"Oh, sure; I got him to talk, about himself," she said. "He has been around quite a lot. Worked for several railroads and some mining interests. His last job, I understood, was with a railroad over in Georgia, the M. and Y."

Slade's eyes narrowed slightly. "The M. and Y." he repeated.

"I'm sure that's what he said," Marie replied. "Well, how did I do?"

"You did wonderfully," he assured her. "Even better than I hoped."

She shot him a glance but asked no questions. He'd talk when he was ready to.

"I told you he'd spill everything once she turned her wolf loose on him," the sheriff chuckled.

"Oh, I flatter myself that I can get any man to talk, especially about himself," Marie returned blithely. "Even you, my dear," she said to Slade.

"Not on the dance floor," he countered smilingly.

The sheriff chuckled. Marie giggled, and changed the subject.

Suddenly she whisked out of her chair and scampered across the room to the orchestra platform, where she engaged the leader in conversation. He nodded vigorously and seized a guitar. Marie trotted back to Slade's table.

"Darling, you've got to sing for us," she said. "Like you did in Miguel's cantina in Laredo. I won't take no for an answer. Come along, now, like a good *muchacho*."

The orchestra leader was waving the guitar beseechingly. Sheriff Ord seconded the request.

"Well, seeing as you did me a real big favor tonight, I guess it's up to me to reciprocate," Slade said.

He arose and walked to the platform. The leader turned to the crowd, which, sensing something out of the ordinary was giving him full attention.

"*Señoritas* and *señors*, silence, please!" he boomed. "*Capitan* will sing."

Conversation sank to a hum, ceased altogether as Slade accepted the guitar and stepped to the edge of the platform. He flashed the white smile of El Halcon, threw back his black head and sang.

104

Upon some of earth's chosen is bestowed the golden gift of glorious song. Walt Slade had that kind of a voice, and as his great metallic baritone-bass thundered through the room, the bartenders stopped pouring, men stood with untasted drinks in their hands, the roulette wheels ceased spinning, the dealers let the cards lie untouched, the dancers stood motionless, hugging partners closer.

Songs of the range he sang for the cowhands. Ballads of the "high iron" for the railroaders. A wistfully beautiful love song, of his own composition, for the girls.

Songs of the hills and the valleys, of the rivers and the plains. Simple little songs, but gems of beauty by the magic of a truly great voice.

He smiled at Marie, whose lashes were already misted with tears, and then:

"Dawn! and the wings of the morning,
The Texas bluebells a-bloom,
But a scarlet leaf breathes a warning
Of the Frost King's kiss, coming soon.
Dusk! And the gold of the twilight.
Night! And the vespers are still.
And on and on, flowing star-bright,
The trial that winds over the hill!"

The music ceased with a crash of chords from the guitar. And the roar of applause that followed quivered the rafters.

"The singingest man in the whole dadblamed Southwest!" somebody exclaimed.

"And with the fastest gunhand!" chortled somebody else.

"And the best boss a man ever worked for," added a railroader. "Hurrah for the Old Man!"

When Slade returned to his table, Marie sighed,

"What chance has a girl got when he sings!"

"Oh, he'd get by if he couldn't warble a note," said the sheriff. "Let us drink!"

Marie returned to the floor. The sheriff, tired of sitting still, was wandering about, passing a word here and there. Slade sat with his coffee and cigarette, thinking deeply.

His thoughts dealt with two men: Morris Thomas and Neale Graham, his assistant and mathematician. Slade had already arrived at certain conclusions relative to the pair.

Thomas was a capable man but, as Packy Maclain had observed, he was easygoing, inclined to think the best of everybody. Graham was the stronger personality. While presumably occupying a subordinate position, he dominated the engineer, though seeming to defer to him. Thomas would accept without question any suggestion he might make.

Shrewd, too. His immediate insistence on shouldering the blame for the "mistake" made concerning the grading of the cut and the direction followed by the tunnel, which Slade had uncovered; this was a sample of his canniness.

Graham was responsible, all right, but not in the manner he led Thomas to believe.

106

Well, thanks to Marie, who was just a little shrewder than Graham, Slade now knew exactly where the mathematician stood. Evidently enamoured of the girl, he had allowed her to persuade him to talk of himself, mentioning responsible positions he had held, with the view of impressing her. And had unwittingly given Slade the lead he needed, when he mentioned to her his previous connection with the M. & Y. Railroad.

For Slade knew that the M. & Y. was a feeder line owned and controlled by the M. K. System!

The M.K.! Jaggers Dunn's opponent in the race to tap the virgin territory to the west, with highly lucrative mail and express contracts also at stake.

And there was not the slightest doubt in Slade's mind but that Graham had been "planted" with the C. & P. to do everything he could to slow up the project. And was presumably also responsible for the criminal acts committed in the section.

"Nice reasoning, very nice," he told his coffee cup. "But how about a little proof with which to back it up? Unfortunately for our side, the proof at present is conspicuous for its nonexistence. The only thing we have against *amigo* Graham is his admission to Marie that he formerly worked for the M. and Y. Railroad. Which, it being a free country, he had a perfect right to do. He could deny any dealings with the M. K. and make it stick."

So the situation stood. With the absolute authority Jaggers Dunn had given him, he could discharge Graham and get rid of him as a hindrance to the C. & P. project. But first and foremost he was a Texas Ranger, and if

Graham was guilty of criminal acts, as Slade firmly believed he was, it was his duty as a Ranger to apprehend him and bring him to justice.

Well, at least now he knew for sure on whom to keep an eye. He could see plainly that ahead of him was not only a battle of guns, very probably, but a battle of wits as well, and Neale Graham would without doubt prove a formidable opponent.

Marie joined him for a few minutes; noted his abstracted expression.

"Still thinking about Mr. Graham?" she asked.

"Yes, I was," he conceded. "And I wish to mention something. You were a great help tonight, confirming my conclusions, and I think he'll be back to see you. Which is all right, only be very careful in all your dealings with him; don't let him realize you are leading him on. He is a dangerous man."

Marie was silent for a moment, evidently turning the warning over in her mind. She glanced around; lowered her voice.

"Is he *the* man?"

"So I have concluded," Slade replied. Marie did not appear surprised.

"Anyhow, it is wonderful to be able to help you, dear," she said softly.

"You always have been," he said. "And I greatly, greatly appreciate it."

"Which is all the reward I ask," she replied, her voice even softer.

Across the table their hands met, in a clasp of perfect understanding.

Suddenly there was a roar that shook the rafters and ground the shingles together.

"Good heavens!" Marie gasped. "What a man!"

It was indeed quite a man who filled the doorway with his bulk. He glanced around and let out another roar. Straight for Slade's table he plowed, a bunch of cowhands stringing after him.

Mack Ware and his floor men rushed forward to try and prevent murder or mayhem. Then they halted in amazement as Buck Hardy, for it was he, flung both arms around Slade and gave him a bear hug, his cowboys grinning and bobbing.

"The best dadblamed man in Texas!" boomed Buck, patting Slade's shoulder. "Anybody who 'lows different will please step up and I'll turn him inside out like a glove!"

He stared and blinked at Marie. "Good gosh!" he whooped. "Didn't expect to see an angel in the Crow Bait."

"Shut up, you loco idjut!" bawled another voice almost as loud as Buck's. "Do you want the lady to bust that bottle over your dadblamed head?"

Marie trilled laughter. Slade waved to old Hans Ragnal, who was bringing up the rear. The Slash H owner shoved Buck aside and flopped into a chair.

"Service!" he bellowed. "Drinks for all of us! Name your pizen, folks. How are you, Slade? Nice to see you again. Hoped we'd find you here."

The Slash H cowboys all shook hands with Slade and then trooped to the bar, where astonishment reigned. Hardy stayed where he was.

"Don't mind Buck, Miss," old Hans said, jerking his head toward his grinning range boss. "He can't help the way he's made. A cuss sent upon me for my sins." He lowered his voice and spoke soberly, addressing Slade.

"Thought it would be a notion to come in and show folks we're on good terms with the railroad," he said. "I've talked with some of the other owners and they'll string along with me."

"That is mighty fine of you, sir," Slade replied. "Marie, this is Mr. Hans Ragnal I mentioned to you."

"Don't mind me, either," Ragnal said. "There's no fool like an old fool, but even an old fool can sometimes mend his ways, with a little prodding. So please don't think too hard of us."

"I think you are all just about the nicest people I've met here yet," Marie declared energetically.

Ragnal turned to Slade, and his hot old eyes were all of a sudden a trifle misty.

"Son," he said, "she sorta reminds me of — *her*."

And Slade knew he was referring to the original of the crayon portrait that hung in his ranch-house living room.

"Marie," he said, his voice all music, "you have just received a very, very nice compliment."

"Thank you, Mr. Ragnal," the girl replied. And her beautiful eyes were understanding. Old Hans bowed his head.

The drinks arrived. Buck let out a whoop of appreciation and the mood of the others lightened.

Marie took a few sips of her wine and then said, "I'll have to get back on the floor; not enough girls to go

110

around tonight, and I mustn't impose on Mr. Ware's good nature."

It was somewhat obvious that big Buck was not particularly versed in the social niceties, but he possessed an instinctive native courtesy that prompted him to do the right thing; he turned to Slade.

"Mind if she hoofs it with me, Mr. Slade?"

"Not in the least, if the lady is willing," the Ranger replied.

"That is unless you want to —" Buck began.

Slade shook his head. "Right now I'd prefer to relax here with Mr Ragnal," he replied.

"Come on, Buck," Marie said. "We'll leave these two nice old gentlemen to their drinks and their smokes. Come along!"

Buck boomed laughter again and led her to the floor where he quickly proved he was no mean dancer.

"She works here?" Ragnal remarked interrogatively, a note of surprise in his voice.

Thinking it best he should know, Slade gave a brief resumé of Marie Telo's background and how she happened to be dancing in the Crow Bait.

"And the orchestra boys who remembered you from Laredo knew you planned to coil your twine here for a spell," Ragnal remarked. "Hmmm! I think I understand. Well, you're both nice people and I like to see nice people get together."

Slade smiled, and did not differ.

"Look at Buck!" Ragnal added. "He's got her in stitches with his loco chatter. He's all right 'cept he's got too much temper and always on the lookout for trouble. Good for him that he ran up against a better man than he is — been a mite subdued of late. He sets up to be quite a fighter."

"He would be, were it not for one thing," Slade replied.

"How's that?" Ragnal asked.

"He loses his temper, which clouds the judgment and lays him wide open to a man who doesn't and who can use his hands."

"Uh-huh, use 'em so they hit like the kick of a mule," old Hans said dryly. "Buck told me confidentially that he never did see where your hands came from when you walloped him."

Slade smiled, and changed the subject.

Sheriff Ord, who had been an interested observer of all that went on, strolled over to join them.

"Howdy, Ben," greeted Ragnal. "Take a load off your feet and down a snort."

"Don't mind if I do, Hans," Ord accepted as he sat down.

"Waiter!" called Ragnal.

While they were discussing the drinks, Morris Thomas entered. Slade caught the engineer's eye and beckoned him to the table, where he and Ragnal were introduced.

At first, Thomas was somewhat diffident, perhaps a trifle fearful as to what reception he would get from the cattleman. But after a bit, he and Ragnal discovered mutual acquaintances over East and their conversation became animated.

At the bar, Slade noted that the Slash H hands and some railroaders were clinking glasses and appeared to be on the best of terms.

So far, so good. He felt he had accomplished something in bringing the two factions together. But his main problem still confronted him. Where would Neale Graham strike next? That he would strike, and soon, Slade was convinced, and earnestly hoped to anticipate his move, which might well be again accompanied by murder. Graham was a killer, no doubt as to that. His philosophy was simple — if your enemy is in your way, remove him without compunction. Which same applied to anybody he might consider an obstruction.

Buck Hardy danced a couple of numbers with Marie, then moseyed to the bar to join his hands. Studying the bar, Slade felt that one or two individuals there were puzzled by the development, and not pleased.

He admitted, however, that it might be but the figment of an over-active imagination.

The night wore on, rowdy and noisy, but without untoward incident. Finally old Hans glanced at the clock and let out a beller; "All right, boys, one more and we're ambling; work to do."

A little later they all streamed out, shouting their goodbyes. Thomas also departed. Sheriff Ord shook his head resignedly.

"Don't know how you did it, but you did," he said to Slade. "Here comes your gal, and I've a notion she is in favor of calling it a night, too."

"Well, what do you think of your new gentleman friend?" he asked.

"I like him," Marie replied. "He's uproariously funny and thinks Walt is tops in everything. The other boys seem nice, too."

"A rowdy bunch, but I figure them dependable in a pinch, Buck especially," said Ord. "Wouldn't you say so, Walt?"

"Yes," the Ranger agreed. "When Buck Hardy gives his friendship it is for better or worse, and he'll never waver. Same goes for old Hans, in my opinion."

"Well, the crowd is thinning out and Ware's shooin' the girls off the floor," Ord said. "Guess we might as well call it a night."

Marie seconded the motion and scampered off to the dressing room.

CHAPTER
TWELVE

The following afternoon, after a short talk with Sheriff Ord, Slade repaired to a general store, where he purchased a small bull's-eye lantern. Making sure it was filled with oil, he stowed it in his saddle pouch.

"I've a notion we may need the darn thing if I find over at the west side of the ridge what I expect to find," he told Shadow as he cinched up. "And I believe I'll have the answer as to why Graham veered the prospective tunnel to the north, as shown on the original plat. Well, perhaps we'll be able to substantiate my hunch, and if it turns out what I think it is, it can prove highly important. Let's go, horse, we got things to do."

When he reached the cutting, he found the work proceeding apace; evidently the promise of a bonus for additional footage was causing the boys to stir their stumps.

Everywhere he was greeted cordially with grins and hand wavings as he rode to the head of the cut and gazed at the cliff face. Here the cutting was deep, as deep as was practicable, he decided. He located Terence Flaherty.

"Tomorrow, start driving the tunnel," he told the foreman. "Deepening the cut more will be but a waste of time and labor. Follow the directional line carefully and keep checking with Mr. Thomas. We don't want any mistakes, for they could prove costly in more ways than one."

"There won't be one, sir, I can promise you that," Flaherty replied. "Both Mr. Thomas and me will be right on the job every foot of the way."

"I don't doubt it," Slade said. "Is Mr. Thomas at the office?"

"Think he is," Flaherty answered. "He was just a little while ago."

Slade found Thomas in the office and acquainted him with his decision to start the bore the following day. Thomas agreed that it was time and promised to keep a careful directional check.

Leaving the cut, Slade rode up the trail to the notch and continued to the western slope. On the lip of the slope he reined in and sat studying the terrain beyond, visioning it as it had been some millions of years before.

Instead of wide grass lands was a vast lake or inland sea, surrounded on all sides by towering mountains. On its verge, strange creatures fed on the unbelievably luxuriant vegetation; mighty saurians, some of them a full ninety feet in length.

They fought there on the edge of the inland sea, rending and tearing with great teeth and claws, until they were drenched in blood, but with no signs of pain or exhaustion, for their slow, reptilian natures cared nothing for wounds.

116

And on all sides, the grim mountains looked down cynically on this petty fray, and bided their time.

The scene changed. The mountains were no longer quiescent. They spouted smoke and flame, hurling huge chunks of red-hot rock into the air, and millions of tons of ash that would fantastically color sun and moon and stars for years to come.

The mountains to the south were shattered, rent asunder, and through the wide openings roared the waters of the lake, draining away, until all that remained was the naked bottom.

The monsters died for want of food and other creatures took their place as grass clothed the old lake bottom; creatures that evolved into the familiar ones known to man.

And now before Walt Slade's eyes stretched the peaceful plain, awaiting the man-made thunders soon to come.

"Enough of day-dreaming," he chuckled to Shadow. "Let's get down to business."

With which he put the big black to the slope and descended to the level ground and turned north to the stream.

When he reached it, he found what he expected to find; that it flowed from an opening in the base of the cliff, which was something less than a score of feet in height and which the stream almost filled from side to side.

Almost, but not quite. Along its south edge, little more than a foot above the surface, was a ledge about two yards in width. Quite likely in times of flood the water flowed over it.

Slade drew rein at the mouth of the cave and lit the bull's-eye lantern. With the beam questing out ahead, he sent Shadow into the bore, watchful of possible pitfalls or other obstructions.

However, the ledge continued, its surface smooth, slowly curving to the south as it followed the course of the stream. Which, incidentally, was also what El Halcon expected.

But where the sunlight pouring in the mouth of the cave began to fade and the ledge widened to a niche a few feet in length, he drew rein; studied the prospect ahead. He dismounted, easing Shadow into the niche.

"The surface ahead doesn't look too good," he explained to the horse. "Sort of broken. So we won't take any chance on your legs. I'll go it on foot from here on. You stay put and keep quiet."

Shadow didn't promise, but Slade figured, correctly, that he could be depended on to obey orders. He strode on, carefully studying the shattered surface of the ledge, concluding it was safe enough and not likely to give way and dunk him in the creek.

For several hundred yards he progressed, with the ledge and the stream still steadily curving to the south. Then abruptly both straightened out to run due east. He continued for a couple of hundred yards, then paused and turned the lantern beam down on the stream.

Black as ink, smooth as glass it lay, seemingly without motion — for no ripple marred its placid surface — but flowing silently between its rocky banks. And it was undoubtedly deep. He noted that the side wall of the cave was scored by crevices, some of them quite large.

For some minutes he stood, estimating the distance he had covered, carefully plotting in his mind the stream's curvature to the south.

"Very clever, *Señor* Graham," he apostrophized the mathematician. "Very very clever, and you came close to putting it over. You're even smarter than I have given you credit for being. Yes; close, but not quite close enough."

For several more minutes he stood thinking. Rolling and lighting a cigarette, he enjoyed a leisurely smoke. Pinching out the butt and tossing it into the stream, he began slowly retracing his steps.

He had almost reached the niche where he had placed his horse when he suddenly halted, snapping the slide over the lantern beam.

Shadow was blowing softly through his nose!

It was something Slade had learned never to ignore. The horse had heard a sound not even his amazingly acute ears could catch.

And abruptly there was something else El Halcon had learned never to ignore, fantastic though it might seem.

In men who ride much alone with danger as a constant stirrup companion, there births and grows a subtle sixth sense that warns of peril when none apparently exists. And in Walt Slade that instinct was highly developed.

CHAPTER
THIRTEEN

Slade hesitated a moment, then silently slipped the lantern into the niche, hesitated again. A cloud had drifted across the sun and the cave was quite gloomy. He eased ahead to where he could see around the curve.

The cloud passed. Sunlight blazed into the cave, revealing two men, gun in hand, stealing cautiously up the bore. It also revealed Slade in its reddish glare.

A startled exclamation, a yelp of warning! Slade hurled himself sideways, drew and shot with both hands. Answering lead stormed about him, showering him with rock fragments, ripping the crown of his already much abused hat, fanning his face as he ducked and weaved. A slug caromed off the heel of his boot, nearly knocking him into the stream. He caught his balance, squeezed both triggers.

A gasping cry echoed the reports, and a gurgling shriek. Slade, still weaving, peered ahead through the powder fog.

Both men were down, one lying motionless. The other thrashed about on the rock floor, screaming chokingly, blood pulsing from his bullet-torn throat. He stiffened; his chest rose mightily as he fought for air, sunk in. It did not rise again.

Automatically reloading, Slade gazed intently at the cave mouth. Nothing appeared against the glow of the sun. He could hear no sound. Looked like there were no more of the devils around. He glided forward, stepping over the two bodies, reached the entrance and again stood motionless, peering and listening. Taking a chance, he stepped out, guns ready for instant action.

The only living things that met his gaze were two saddled and bridled horses standing nearby, which regarded him with mild, questioning eyes.

For several minutes he stood scanning the terrain in every direction. Satisfied there were no more drygulchers lurking about, he stripped the rigs from the horses, re-entered the cave and made his way to where Shadow waited.

"Well, horse, I slipped," he told the big black. "And if it hadn't been for you letting me know I had, it might well have been a fatal slip. Your ears and your nose-blowing made the difference. Was close, anyhow, darn close. I slipped a little again when I walked around that bulge and right into the sunlight when the cloud passed.

"And I should have realized that the cunning devil was keeping tabs on my every move. He figured what I would very likely do, or decided that at least there might be an opportunity for a drygulching, and sent a couple of his sidewinders to do the chore. Must be always some of them within call. No, he doesn't miss many bets. Guess he didn't think to count on you. Well,

122

it all worked out, so I can't complain. We'll leave those bodies right as they are and hightail to town and notify Sheriff Ord. Better than an hour until sundown, so we should have plenty of time."

Leading Shadow out of the cave, the big black deftly skirting the two dead men sprawled on the floor, he stowed the lantern away, mounted and headed for Redmon at a fast pace, not drawing rein until he reached the sheriff's office, where he found Ord and Deputy Hal Boone.

"Figured you should be showing up soon," said the sheriff. "Let's have it."

Slade told them, briefly. Ord wasted no time with needless questions.

"Hal, tie onto a couple of pack mules — those outlaw critters may have strayed — and follow us," he told the deputy. "Okay, Walt, all set to go."

As they rode, Slade briefed the sheriff on the details of the incident.

"I made the inexcusable blunder of underestimating Graham," he concluded. "Guess my mind was so full of what I expected to find in that cave that I forgot about him."

"And you did find what you expected to?" Ord asked.

"Yes," Slade replied. "And Graham found it before I did. If the original plat had been followed, the tunnel would have tapped that underground river and flooded both tunnel and cut from end to end. And incidentally, very likely would have drowned some workers. Anyhow, we would have had a sweet chore of damming it and pumping out. Would have delayed the project for weeks. Well, thanks largely to Shadow, it didn't work."

"And also because you caught on in time, after looking things over," Ord added. "Well, old man Dunn is sure indebted to you."

"And a great many people, some who don't even know it, are indebted to him for kindnesses and consideration," Slade said. "He sets up to be a tough old jigger, and he can be tough when necessary, but there's a little known side to him that is mighty soft where folks in trouble or in need of help are concerned. The average person would never guess it, for he never talks about such acts on his part. He's a real hombre. Well, here we are, and those horses are still hanging around, but we'll wait till Boone arrives with the mules. You can tie onto those critters and we'll take them to town with us; good nags and should bring a pretty fair price; guess the county treasury won't lose anything, especially when what you'll probably find in the pockets of those two horned toads is added."

The bodies were examined and did divulge a fair amount of money but nothing else Slade considered of importance.

"Nope, no rock dust in the pocket seams," Slade replied to a question from the sheriff. "This pair never worked in the cutting, I'd say. Well, we might as well take it easy and wait for Boone."

They didn't have to wait long. Shortly, the deputy arrived with the mules. The bodies were loaded, the outlaw horses bridled and they headed for Redmon through the velvety gold of the twilight.

124

As they climbed the slope, Slade slid his Winchester from the boot and rested it across the saddle in front of him. He thought there was little danger of an attempt being made against them but was taking no chances. Not with that canny devil who had so frequently proven his ingenuity and his capacity for doing the unexpected.

However, they reached town without untoward happening. The bodies were laid out in the office and the usual gathering of the curious viewed them, with negative results.

Which did not concern Slade much. He knew his man, and with whom his followers might have associated mattered little.

Finally the sheriff got rid of the crowd and shut the door. The horses had already been cared for and Boone was looking after the mules.

"So I guess we might as well go eat," said Ord. "Wonder if Graham will show up tonight?"

"I rather think he will," Slade replied. "He appears to be somewhat impressed by Marie, and will likely wish to see her again."

"Think he has any notion you have caught onto him?"

"I really doubt it," Slade said. "I think his conceit is so great that he figures he is able to keep in the clear. Of course he has me tagged as Dunn's trouble-shooter and, I'd say, thinks I'm really interested only in the progress of the construction work. Which is a logical assumption on his part; I think he believes he convinced me that the original lines and estimates were an honest mistake that anybody could make. He's right about that, incidentally; competent and trustworthy engineers have made similar ones. Well, let's get moving. First I wish to buy a pair of boots. These are pretty well worn and the left one hasn't much heel left. A slug, fortunately travelling low, took off most of it and nearly dunked me in the creek."

"Place right around the corner on Main Street will fix you up," said the sheriff. "Let's go."

The chore was taken care of; the new boots were satisfactory.

"Charge it to the county," said Ord, "and a new hat, too, that one is sorta airy."

"Pays to be shot at," Slade smiled as the new headgear was produced.

"Uh-huh, if all that's punctured are hats and boots," the sheriff qualified the statement. "Now you look better, less like a range tramp."

"We have some very nice new belts, Sheriff, large sizes; how about a little business with you?" suggested the salesman.

"And that'll be enough out of *you*," replied the peace officer. "Come along, Walt, 'fore we get insulted some more."

The clerk chuckled and cordially wished them goodnight, which was returned in kind.

The evening was getting along and they found the Crow Bait busy, the girls already on the floor. Marie joined them for a moment.

"Oh, sure, we heard about it," she said. "Deputy Boone came in a little while ago and told us. A monotonous sameness. As I said before, you couldn't walk out the door without getting into trouble."

"Just so he gets out again in one piece," the sheriff replied cheerfully. "Waiter!"

Slade's earlier prediction was justified; Neale Graham did appear, his usual urbane self. He paused at the table for a moment.

"Hear you had another stirring adventure today, Mr. Slade, and came out of it unscathed," he said. "Congratulations! A little more of the good work and perhaps we'll have peace hereabouts for a change."

With a smile and a nod, he moved to the dance floor as the number ceased. A few moments later he was dancing with Marie.

"You know, I've a notion that hellion is snickerin' at us up his sleeve," growled the sheriff. "He'll laugh on the other side of his face 'fore the last brand is run."

"Hope so," Slade agreed. "No guarantee that he will, though; he's a slippery customer."

"Notice he didn't mention anything about the underground river," Ord observed.

"Naturally," Slade replied. "He's not supposed to know anything about it. To mention it would be a give-away that he does. He never misses a bet."

Which evoked another growl from the sheriff, and a savage attack on his dinner. Slade laughed and approached his helpin' in a more leisurely manner.

Graham had three dances with Marie; then bought wine and sat with her at a table for a while.

"He's smitten with her, all right," said the sheriff.

"But not seriously," Slade differed. "He finds her interesting, but I don't think he would allow feeling for any woman to interfere with his plans. He's playing for big stakes and that is paramount where he is concerned."

A little later, Graham rose to his feet, waved goodnight to Slade and the sheriff and departed.

Marie did not at once join them. Instead, she danced a couple of numbers with other patrons.

"Why doesn't she come over?" wondered Ord.

"Because she's smart," Slade replied. "She knows better than to make it obvious that she is reporting to us what Graham had to say to her, against the chance that somebody is keeping tabs."

"By gosh, I believe you're right!" the sheriff exclaimed admiringly. "Yep, a plumb smart gal."

After the second number was finished, Marie did join them, pausing on her way across the room with several occupants of tables.

"Well," she said as she sat down and accepted a glass of wine, "well, Mr. Graham is in love."

The sheriff didn't look surprised. Slade only smiled slightly and prompted, "Yes?"

"Yes," the girl replied. "He's very much in love with — himself. That's all he talked about, showing only the slightest of interest in my unworthy self. Merely asked, in an absentminded manner, if I planned to be here long, then went back to his original subject. Mentioning other outfits with which he had worked, hinting broadly that he held very responsible positions with them. He said he hopes and expects promotion with the C. and P."

"He said that?" Slade said thoughtfully.

"That's right," Marie returned, sipping her wine.

"And what did he mean by that?" asked Ord.

"It means, for one thing," Slade answered soberly, "that it's up to me to keep a sharper eye on Morris Thomas. If something happened to Thomas, Graham would be his logical successor."

"Whe-e-ew!" said Ord. "Looks like you might be right there, too."

"It also means, I would say," Slade added, "for which I am glad, that he hasn't tumbled to the fact that I suspect him. As I said earlier in the evening, he is so sure of himself that he believes he has covered up perfectly. Well, that weakness may prove his undoing."

"When he said that about promotion, there was a look in his eyes that sort of gave me the shivers," Marie continued. "I don't think I'm the scary type, but I'm afraid of him. He did something, too, that didn't help.

"A fly was buzzing around. He knocked it down with his hand — he moves like a flash — and while it was struggling on the table, he picked it up and deliberately tore off its legs and its wings."

"The ornery blankety-blank!" growled the sheriff.

Marie didn't take him to task for his language. In fact, she looked as if she approved.

"Yes, he undoubtedly has a sadistic streak," Slade said. "And, I'd say, he is afflicted with the blood lust. I'd hate to fall into his hands."

Marie shuddered.

129

"Don't worry, he won't," Ord assured her. "It'll end up the other way around, what's left of him, which won't be enough to bother about."

"I hope so," the girl replied. "Such people have no right to live."

"My sentiments," said the sheriff. "Let us drink."

The Crow Bait was booming, and so were the streets and, presumably all the other saloons.

"Never changes," snorted Ord. "And payday is right around the corner. Then you'll really see something."

"I'm looking forward to it," Marie said, with a giggle.

The sheriff indulged in another snort, and addressed himself to his drink.

The Crow Bait was noisy and boisterous, but everybody appeared in a good temper and enjoying themselves. Marie returned to the dance floor. Slade and the sheriff sat on at their, table, smoking and talking. The latter glanced around and shook his head.

"Plumb peaceful, so far," he remarked. "Too good to last. Betcha something busts loose somewhere before closing time. Listen to those drunks on the street whooping it up. Well, guess as long as they don't do anything worse than yelp and sing — or try to — we can't complain. Maybe we will get through the night without trouble."

However, the sheriff was something of an optimist, as coming events would tend to prove.

CHAPTER
FOURTEEN

The Comstock saloon on Park Avenue was also doing a booming business. The bar was packed, most of the tables occupied. The two husky floor men were keeping a watch on a pair of customers in cowhand garb who were arguing rather angrily about something. However, it appeared to be nothing worse than a word fight, so the floor men didn't pay them too much mind.

In the back room, with both doors shut and locked, Grimshaw, the owner, sat at a table covered with money which he was counting. The door of an old iron safe stood open, ready to receive the week's take, a large sum, which on the morrow would be sent east via train and banked, there being no such establishment in Redmon, so far, although there was talk that one would be set up in the near future.

Suddenly from the outer room sounded yells and curses and a crashing of overturned chairs. Grimshaw leaped to his feet and started to cross the room to the saloon door.

But even as he did so, the alley door behind him crashed open. Two masked men bounded in. Grimshaw whirled and make a grab for a gun in the table drawer. Before he could reach it, the barrel of another gun, wielded by one of the intruders, crashed down on his skull to stretch him on the floor, bleeding and senseless.

In the saloon, the floor men were wrestling two cursing combatants apart and rushing them to the swinging doors. The task proved singularly easy, for the battlers put up very little resistance. Outside, they weaved down the street, still waving their arms and swearing at each other. The floor men dusted off their hands and returned to the saloon. One glanced at the closed door to the back room.

"Funny the boss didn't come out," one remarked. "He must have heard that ruckus. Guess he figured we'd be able to handle things."

The other nodded agreement and they turned their attention elsewhere.

Meanwhile in the back room, the two intruders had picked up the money from the table and stuffed it into a sack one carried.

From the alley sounded a low whistle. Without a glance at the unconscious Grimshaw, the two robbers hurried to the alley door. The two "fighting drunks" loomed before them, leading horses.

"All set?" one asked. "Okay, let's go."

Fast hoofs clicked up the alley. On the back room floor, the Comstock owner lay motionless, blood still oozing from his split scalp.

Some little time passed. Then the head bartender called to the floor men to fetch some stock from the back room. One went to the door, turned the knob, realized it was locked. He hammered on the door. No response. He hammered harder, called out. Still no response.

"What in blazes is the matter with Grimshaw?" he cried peevishly. "Why don't he answer?"

The other floor man was quicker of wit. "Here, help me with this table and bust that damn door open!" he exclaimed. "Something funny about this."

The table was crashed against the door. The lock snapped and the door swung open. One look, and all hell cut loose in the Comstock.

The quick-witted floor man knelt beside Grimshaw, felt of his heart.

"Ain't dead," he called. "But he's bad hurt. Somebody fetch Doc Clay — you'll find him over at the Astor House Hotel. And somebody fetch the sheriff; he'll be at his office or at the Crow Bait, chances are. Get a move on!"

Slade was enjoying a cup of coffee, Ord a drink when a wildly excited man banged through the swinging doors, bawling for the sheriff.

"What the heck's the matter with you?" roared Ord. "What the devil do you want?"

The fellow gabbled forth what he knew of the goings-on at the Comstock. The sheriff spouted profanity.

"Knew it was too good to last!" he stormed. "Come on, Walt, let's see what happened in that rumhole. I *will* close the blankety-blank rat nest!"

"Take it easy," Slade advised. "I don't think there is anything we can do at present. All right, let's go, but don't have a stroke."

The sheriff subsided to rumblings and mutterings and they headed for the Comstock.

When they reached it, both the saloon and the street were crowded. They pushed their way to the back room to find Doc Clay had already arrived from the nearby Astor House and was ministering to the stricken owner. He looked up at their entrance.

"Got a nasty wallop, but there is no fracture, so far as I can ascertain," he said to Slade. "Take a look, Walt, and see what you think; you've got hands that miss nothing."

Slade probed the vicinity of the wound with his sensitive fingertips and agreed with the doctor's diagnosis.

"Of course there may be concussion; we'll learn about that later," Clay observed. "I've given him a stimulant and I think he'll be coming out of it shortly. Then we'll arrange to put him to bed. I gather he lives at the Astor House, too. Somebody rustle something that will do for a stretcher."

Meanwhile, the sheriff was questioning the floor men and the bartenders. From the information he gleaned, Slade quickly reconstructed the crime.

"An old trick, but effective," he said. "Start a phony ruckus at the bar, with plenty of noise, to attract everybody's attention, including that of the floor men, who get busy breaking up the row, with no thought of anything else. Meanwhile, that pair's companion or companions crashed the alley door, knocked out Grimshaw, scooped up the money and hightailed."

134

He crossed the room to the alley door and examined the lock, which was an old fashioned one.

"I could break that cast-iron hasp with a blow of my fist from the outside," he remarked. "Same old story there. Folks think that if a door is locked, that is all that's necessary, which isn't always the case." He turned to the floor men.

"Tomorrow, have a bar put across that door, to drop into good steel or wrought-iron hasps on either side of the door," he directed. "That will make it safe against a possible repeat performance."

"Take care of it first thing, Mr. Slade," the floor man promised. "First thing in the morning."

"Did they get much?" the Ranger asked.

"Plenty," the floor men replied. "A whole week's take."

Slade turned to the sheriff, after a glance at the doctor busy with his patient.

"We might as well stick around until Grimshaw regains consciousness," he said. "Doc has just given him another little shot and he should be snapping out of it before long. Perhaps he'll be able to tell us something."

Grimshaw did respond to the stimulant shortly, but had little to add to what was known.

"I hardly got a glimpse of the devils," he replied to a question from Slade. "The one that walloped me seemed rather big, but that's about all I can say. They wore blue masks. I don't think I'd know them if I happened to see them again without the masks."

The floor men and the bartenders were vague as to the appearance of the pair that had staged the fake row in the saloon, and their descriptions differed.

Grimshaw, with the doctor in attendance, was packed off to bed.

"No inquest this time, but it was close," Clay said cheerfully. "He's got a hard head, but a little farther down the side might well have busted it. Guess he's lucky to be with us. Be seeing you."

As they headed for the Crow Bait, Slade remarked to Ord,

"Well, our *amigo* Graham put one over nicely and made a good haul."

"You figure then it was some of his devils?"

"Of course," Slade replied. "All the earmarks of one of his operations. Concisely planned, carefully executed. He may have even handled the chore himself. The big one who walloped Grimshaw could have been Graham. I believe you told me he was in the habit of hanging out in the Comstock. Got the low-down on everything, learned what day the money would be sent east and made his grab for it the night before. Yes, very smooth. He's quite a gent."

The sheriff swore dismally and said several things not complimentary to *Señor* Neale Graham.

"Well, here we are," he concluded, "and do I need a snort!"

The Crow Bait was buzzing over the robbery when they entered, but not for long, the habituées of that emporium having other matters of more importance to occupy them. Such things were taken as a matter of

136

course in Redmon and occasioned no lasting impression.

"Well, at least you didn't get mixed up in that one, for which I am duly thankful," Marie said to Slade. "Really remarkable you didn't figure it out in advance and be Johnny on the spot."

"I'm not exactly clairvoyant," the Ranger replied smilingly.

"Sometimes I think you are," she differed. "It is perfectly uncanny the way you anticipate things at times."

"And right now I anticipate your desire for a sip of wine," he said, motioning a waiter.

"How's that for the second sight in good working order, Sheriff?" Marie asked. "His Scotch ancestry would be proud of him. Well, this persiflage is entertaining, but I'm glad to see the crowd is thinning out and Mr. Ware is motioning the girls off the floor. I'm tired and anticipate a good night's rest."

"Better consult the 'second sight' about that," the sheriff advised dryly.

Marie made a face at him, finished her wine and scampered off to the dressing room.

CHAPTER
FIFTEEN

When Slade reached the cutting, a little after noon, he found the steam shovels clearing away the rock the blasts set by the night shift had brought down. For Flaherty and Packy Maclain, the night foreman, had done a little "anticipating" themselves.

"Didn't see any sense in waiting until today," Flaherty explained. "So I told Maclain to go ahead and blow 'em. And you sure did figure it right down to the minute, Mr. Slade. We're through the granite and into the shale. Should be easy going from now on, with little waste of powder."

"Yes, we should make real progress from here on, Terence," Slade agreed. "But be very careful with your shoring," he admonished. "We don't want the mountain tumbling down on our heads. Is Mr. Thomas at the office? Okay, I'll have a word with him. See you a little later."

Slade found the engineer busy at his desk. Graham was not present.

"I've checked and rechecked," Thomas said. "Everything appears to be going smoothly. I'm sure Mr. Dunn is going to be very pleased."

"Hope so," Slade replied. "He's very particular. Well, I'm heading back to town for a while. Doc Clay wants to hold an inquest on those two drygulchers, and seeing as I was the only 'witness' to their demise, I'm supposed to be there."

At the beginning of the cut, Slade drew rein and gazed back toward the scene of operations. Yes, everything connected with the project appeared to be progressing smoothly, with no indications otherwise. That is, if the pestiferous Graham didn't manage to toss a monkey wrench into the machinery somehow. He had come close to it several times, and perhaps the law of averages would ultimately react to his advantage.

Well, as the sheriff said, some laws could stand a mite of fracturing, and it was up to him to provide the necessary strain. He rode in a complacent frame of mind.

The inquest didn't take long. Slade was exonerated of wrongdoing and congratulated on coming out of the affair unscathed.

"Plus new boots and a new hat," he observed to the sheriff after the jury had departed and the bodies had been removed — to make room for the next batch, as the sheriff said.

"Figure that pair just packed out were cowhands?" Ord asked.

"They never were," Slade replied, "like several of the others we managed to corral. Certain marks on their hands, however, make me inclined to believe they had been employed quite a bit as construction workers. Lots of those fellows are in the same category as chuck line riding cowhands. I think Graham largely collected his bunch from migrant workers of easy conscience who can ride and shoot, as many of them can, along with a few renegade cowhands. One way or another he manages to keep them well supplied with spending money, so they stick with him and obey orders."

"A few of them haven't managed to stick," the sheriff observed dryly, nodding toward the now vacant floor.

"Yes," Slade conceded, "but I fear he doesn't have great difficulty corraling replacements. Always plenty of that sort following big construction camps. One of the things that plagued General Dodge in the course of the building of the Union Pacific. Those camps were notorious for lawlessness."

"Couldn't have been any worse than this spider nest," growled the sheriff. "Listen to 'em out there, will you! And it's still quite a ways till dark."

"Understand that day after tomorrow is payday," Slade remarked.

"That's right," said Ord. "Then real heck and blazes will cut loose. Well, I've sent for my other deputy to come over from the county seat, and I'm hiring three or four specials, fellers I can depend on. Guess we'll be able to hold the lid down, after a fashion. Anyhow, after what Hans Ragnal told us about the other owners stringing along with him, I figure there won't be any serious trouble between the railroaders and the cowhands. The riders will fall in line with what their bosses decide on, and you will have the railroaders toeing the mark. So I reckon any ruckuses will be personal shindigs, which aren't too hard to handle. Last

140

payday we had a pretty sizeable riot between railroaders and punchers. Don't expect anything like that this time, but there'll be plenty of hell raised once the redeye really begins getting in its licks. You can always figure on that when rambunctious young hellions get to downin' snorts. Difference of opinion over a gal, or cards, or something. Well, we'll see. Now what you got in mind?"

"I'm going to ride back to the cutting and look things over more carefully," Slade replied. "See you a little later."

At the cutting, Flaherty, in accordance with Slade's order, had pulled back many of his men from the tunnel mouth to take over the chore of widening the cut. They were making good progress.

Slade watched the operation for a while, then repaired to the office for a few more words with Thomas. Graham was still not present.

"He wasn't feeling at all well this morning, so I told him to take a couple of days off," the engineer replied to Slade's question as to his whereabouts. "That way he won't need to be on the job until after payday, which is day after tomorrow. He's been working hard and I figure he can stand a little rest."

Slade nodded, was silent for a couple of minutes, then asked another question; "When does the paycar arrive?"

"Tomorrow night," Thomas answered. "Will follow the usual procedure. The scheduled material train will drop it off at Floyd, a bit more than thirty miles to the east of here. It will draw the money from the Floyd bank, where the Company has an account. We'll have an engine and a caboose over there to pick it up and bring it on to Redmon."

Slade was again silent while he rolled and lighted a cigarette. After the brain tablet was functioning to his satisfaction, he asked still another question,

"Does a guard accompany the paymaster?"

"Why, no," the engineer said. "Never figured one would be required. But if you think it wise, we'll dispatch one with the engine."

"I don't think it will be necessary," Slade replied and asked a final question: "What time does the engine leave the yards?"

"About five o'clock, after the second material train clears," the engineer answered. Slade nodded, and changed the subject. After a few more words, dealing with the widening of the cut, he returned to Redmon, his eyes thoughtful.

After stabling Shadow, he watched the sunset flame and fade, and then dropped in at the sheriff's office, where he found Ord declaring it was time to eat.

Neale Graham did not appear at the Crow Bait that evening. When Marie remarked on the fact, Slade repeated, without comment, that Thomas had told him the mathematician was slightly under the weather. Marie regarded him in silence for a moment, then quoted.

"'When the Divil was sick, the Divil a Monk would be. But when the Divil was well, the divil a Monk was he.'"

"Could be," Slade conceded soberly.

142

The following late afternoon found Slade in the yards. He had no difficulty locating the engine and caboose that would pull out shortly for Floyd, to fetch the paycar and the paymaster. He mounted the steps and entered. The conductor, with whom Slade was acquainted, was reading at his little desk. He glanced up as the Ranger entered.

"Why, hello, Mr. Slade," he greeted. "How are you?"

"Fine, Nat," Slade replied. "And you?"

"Couldn't be better," the conductor returned. He glanced expectantly at El Halcon.

"Nat," Slade said, "I'm riding to Floyd with you."

"Fine!" the conductor repeated. "Something in the wind?"

"Frankly, I don't know," Slade admitted. "I just feel like going along, sort of playing a hunch, as it were."

"Understand your hunches usually pay off," chuckled Nat. "Well, nice to have you along, anyhow; makes me feel better. Funny things have happened hereabouts of late."

A short while later the little train pulled out of the yards and headed for Floyd, the engine backing up and shoving the caboose in front of it, for there was no turn-table or "Y" at Floyd, by way of which it could be turned for the trip back to Redmon; only a spur and a couple of sidings.

In consequence, progress was rather slow and dusk was falling when they reached Floyd, where the caboose was coupled to the rear of the paycar, the locomotive hooked on in front, its nose pointing to Redmon.

143

The paycar was an old reconditioned express car with wide side doors, which were locked.

Before the train pulled out, Slade contacted the conductor.

"Nat," he said, "if something should happen between here and Redmon, stay put. Don't under any circumstances leave it. Be best to hit the floor at once, and stay down. And don't, I repeat, leave the caboose until I give you the word."

The conductor looked decidedly startled. "Why — why do you expect something to happen, Mr. Slade?" he asked.

"I repeat what I said before," Slade replied. "Really I don't know, but I figure it best not to take chances. Don't forget, do exactly as I told you. Now I want to see the paymaster."

Nat led the way to the rear end door, on which he knocked. Bolts rattled, the door was opened, to reveal the paymaster, a pleasant appearing elderly man.

"Mr. Slade, this is Mr. Standish, the paymaster," Nat introduced. "Mr. Standish, Mr. Slade is the Big Boss during the absence of Mr. Dunn, and what he says goes." Standish nodded his understanding.

"A pleasure to know you, Mr. Slade," he acknowledged. "Come right in."

"Okay," Slade said. "I'm riding with you from here to Redmon. All right, Nat, let's get going."

The conductor waved a highball. The engineer tooted two blasts, accepting the signal. The train got under way as Standish locked and barred the end door. He glanced inquiringly at El Halcon.

144

"Mr. Standish," Slade answered the implied question, "listen closely to what I tell you." He let the full force of his steady eyes rest on the paymaster's face.

"Mr. Standish," he repeated, "I want you to do exactly what I tell you, with no time wasted asking questions. I'm not sure something will happen, but as I told Nat, best not to take chances. If you fail to obey me without hesitation, your life may well be forfeit."

The paymaster appeared decidedly perturbed, which was not strange, under the circumstances.

"But — but they'd have trouble getting in, with all the doors locked," he said.

"Not at all," Slade replied. "I've encountered somewhat similar circumstances before. The train stopped by something, a stick of dynamite against the side door and it's blown to pieces, and you very likely with it if you happened to be at your desk and right in line. So move your chair over here beside mine at the end door. Never mind locking the safe; if things don't go right with us, it will make no difference whether it's locked or open; they'd have their ways of forcing you to open it, rather unpleasant ways, before a knife was stuck in your back."

Abruptly he laughed. "I'm talking as if it's a foregone conclusion that something will be attempted," he said. "And really, as I said, I'm just playing a hunch. We may make the run peacefully. But better to play it safe than be sorry we didn't. Okay, here you should be safe enough. If a ruckus does cut loose, hit the floor, and stay there."

145

As a matter of fact, Slade was not exactly playing a hunch. His actions were based on the sudden "illness" of Neale Graham and his apparent absence from town. If something were attempted against the large amount of money in the safe, it would assuredly be somewhere along the lonely stretch between Floyd and Condon, where in many places the setup was ideal. With only the train crew and the paymaster to contend with, the possible outlaws would have little difficulty attaining their objective. With them out of the way or held at bay, the desperadoes could take their time rifling the safe and escaping, since the line had been cleared for the paycar and no material train would be due from the east for several hours. Slade rolled a cigarette and settled himself in comfort as the train sped along, the locomotive exhaust purring, the side rods clanking a musical refrain.

They had covered perhaps half the distance to Condon and the right of way was following a wide curve that ran through a stand of tall and thick brush when Slade got his not altogether unexpected warning. Suddenly the exhaust shut off. Brake shoes screeched against the wheels.

"Hang on!" he snapped to the paymaster. "Here we go!"

CHAPTER
SIXTEEN

There was a muffled crash. The paycar leaped and bucked, careening wildly, but stayed on the iron. Outside sounded a crackle of shots. The outlaws were here, all right, shooting at the caboose.

The paymaster didn't have to be told to hit the floor; he was already knocked to it by the impact and stayed there. Slade kept his balance, stood tense and ready.

A booming explosion! The side door flew to pieces. Again the car rocked and swayed.

Through the smoky opening vaulted two men. Slade's voice thundered at them.

"Up! You're covered! In the name of the State of Texas!"

Yelps of alarm, a grabbing for guns. Slade drew and shot with both hands. One of the intruders reeled and fell back through the door. Answering slugs hammered the wall beside the weaving, ducking Ranger. Another blast from the big Colts and the door was cleared; two men sprawled on the ground.

The shooting outside had ceased, replaced by a torrent of curses. A voice shouted an order. There was a crackling of brush, then the thud of fast hoofs fading through the dark to the north.

Slade reasoned that one of the owlhoots, doubtless Neale Graham, had realized that the game was up, with that perception which is part of the mental outfit of the great; for Slade could have killed all of them had they continued trying to crash the paycar.

"Guess that's all," he told the yammering paymaster. "But stay where you are for a minute while I make sure."

He glided to the door, flipped off his hat and eased it around the edge, simulating a man cautiously looking out.

Nothing happened, which did not particularly surprise him. He took a chance, leaped to the ground, instantly shifting his position.

Still nothing happened, and in the darkness, if one of the devils had stayed behind in the hope of getting a shot at him, now he held the advantage. He sped lightly to the edge of the brush and stood listening for several moments. If anybody were holed up in the growth, his keen ears would have caught the sound of his breathing.

"Okay, Nat," he called to the conductor. "You can come out now; everything under control."

With the wildly excited trainmen trooping after him, he made his way to the front of the engine. The engineer and the fireman, who had also hit their deck when the outlaws started shooting, popped into view.

The glare of the headlight showed that several crossties and some earth and stones had been heaped on the track, enough to cause the engineer to instantly close his throttle and apply the brakes when he spotted the obstruction.

Slade examined the front of the locomotive.

"Pilot smashed, but the pony trucks and the drivers are on the iron," he announced. "All the running gear appears unharmed, and the rails are okay. We'll clear this mess out of the way and get going; load those two bodies into the car and we'll pack them with us for the sheriff to look over."

The chores were quickly accomplished and the delayed train got under way.

"Thanks to you, Mr. Slade, the boys will have their payday on schedule," Standish said. "And," he added soberly, "thanks to you, we are all alive and unhurt, which I think we would not have been were it not for you. They strike me as the sort that are not much on leaving witnesses."

"It is possible," Slade conceded. "It's a killer bunch. Fortunately, the advantage was on my side — the element of surprise — and they were caught a trifle off-balance."

"I'd say another explanation could be offered," the paymaster replied in a dry voice.

"You're darn right," put in the conductor. "He's all the time doing things like that. You can always depend on the Old Man doing the right thing at the right time."

"Which evidently Mr. Dunn knows," commented Standish. "And Mr. Dunn seldom makes mistakes."

However, due to the excitement, the paymaster did. make a mistake, neglecting to inform Slade of something; the result of this omission, later, was trouble.

Slade examined the bodies, with no hope that one would prove to be Graham, although he was confident the mathematician had directed the attempt in person, and that it was his voice that had ordered the retreat when he saw the attempt had failed.

Well, not a bad day, everything taken into account, and another setback for *amigo* Graham. But one which, El Halcon soberly reflected, would make him all the more dangerous and lethal.

When the long overdue paycar train boomed into the yard, they found its staff in a state of what Sheriff Ord would have characterized as the jitters, and the relief of all parties concerned was profound.

Explanations were in order, which Standish and the train crew supplied without reservation for the benefit of the crowd, which was constantly augmented by fresh arrivals. When the account was finished, there arose a roar from the assembled workers which was perhaps growing repetitious but was nevertheless wholehearted;

"Hurrah for the Old Man!"

Sheriff Ord took charge of the bodies, which he ordered packed to his office, where Slade joined him.

"I sent Boone to tell your gal you're all right," he said. "She was developin' a prize case of the jitters when you didn't show up and that blasted train, neither. Of course we figured you were with it.

"Well, what do you think?" he asked, after the office was finally cleared of the curious, several of whom were certain they had seen the two outlaws in town at one time or another.

"For one thing," Slade replied, "this pair were formerly cowhands. Would appear Graham recruits from all ranks.

"But," he added, "I've a feeling that he is running short of man power. I'm pretty sure there were but three horses hightailed away from the right of way and there is no doubt in my mind but that Graham himself was one of them. That would leave him but a couple of followers if I figure the situation correctly. However, Graham is a host unto himself. Besides, there is no guarantee but that he can tie onto some more hellions if he's of a mind to."

"I'd say," put in the sheriff, "that you've got him on the run. Wouldn't be surprised if he might pull out."

"Not yet, I'd say," Slade differed. "I expect he still has an ace or two up his sleeve. I feel pretty sure he has something real smart in mind that will tend to slow up the project. What, I haven't the slightest notion, but you can wager that if he does pull some sort of a caper, it'll be smooth."

"Think the paycar is safe in the yards?" Ord asked.

"Custer's cavalry couldn't tie onto what's in that car tonight," Slade replied. "Half the force are guarding it, including the night shift, which isn't working and which will sleep with one eye open. Don't worry about the paycar. Well, I am in favor of the Crow Bait and a surrounding; been quite a while since breakfast."

They walked past the yards, just for a look. Everywhere could be seen shadowy figures moving about, and quite likely in the darker nooks there were others that did not move about.

"Boys are taking no chances on missing out on their payday bust," chuckled the sheriff.

When they reached the Crow Bait, they found Marie in a resigned frame of mind and looking forward to the payday bust.

"Perhaps you quieted down those devils enough to hold over for a day or two," she said to Slade. "I sure hope so. I can stand just a little normal excitement for a change."

"You'll get it tomorrow, but I ain't promising it'll be what most folks would call normal," predicted the sheriff. "There'll be heck raisin' aplenty, enough to even satisfy you."

Marie laughed, and trotted off to the floor.

While they were eating, Morris Thomas arrived and accepted a drink.

"Well, Mr. Slade, if you didn't have them already, you've sure got the boys solid behind you," he said. "They would have been mighty low if their bust had been delayed. Been looking forward to it for a month. Would have been a shame were it put off till some more money was obtained."

"How's Graham?" Slade asked casually.

"All right, I guess," the engineer replied. "I stopped at the place where he stays but didn't get any answer to my knock. Guess he was out getting a breath of fresh air."

152

Slade felt that after sniffing powder smoke uncomfortably close, Graham very likely did welcome a little untainted air.

With things in a state of expectant suspension, as it were, business was quite slack, the Crow Bait closed early and everybody called it a night.

CHAPTER
SEVENTEEN

The weather gods had evidently decided to cooperate to make payday a success, for the morning dawned bright and clear, with just enough wind to temper the heat and raise swirls of dust in the streets that soon would be hammered by the hoofs of cow ponies and the brogans of the construction workers.

Ord's other deputy arrived from the county seat and the sheriff swore in his four specials.

"Guess they should be able to handle anything less than a full-fledged riot, which this time I hardly expect, seeing as the railroaders and the cowhands are bunkies now, thanks to you," he observed to Slade. "Just some friendly head whackin' and nose bustin' I expect will be all. Well, guess the hellions have some fun coming to 'em. Hope I ain't being too blasted optimistic, as you'd say."

Slade did not commit himself, for in such a town as Redmon, the unexpected could be expected. He fortified himself with a good breakfast, over which he lingered.

Soon cowhands from the nearer spreads began arriving. And a little later the paycar window was opened and a long line of workers began filing past.

Saloons and shops made ready to reap the golden harvest.

Doc Clay held his usual inquest, with the usual verdict, the sheriff snorting disgustedly at such a waste of time.

"Should do some business today or tonight," Doc observed cheerfully before ambling out.

"Old coot may be nearer the truth than he realizes," Ord remarked. "This is sure going to be a humdinger, what with the regular pay those hellions pull down, plus the bonus you're giving them."

"They've earned it," Slade said. "They sure have been knocking out the work."

"They're stirrin' their stumps more to please you than for the extra money," Ord replied. "As Flaherty said, they'd follow you to hell and back. And they trust you to be for them, first, last and always."

"Which poses a heavy responsibility," Slade said soberly.

Slade and the sheriff kept a close watch on the various places as more and more workers streamed into town. To the Crow Bait and the Comstock they gave little mind, for both were run strictly on the up-and-up; however, it was different with some of the rumholes, as the sheriff characterized them.

However, the appearance of El Halcon and the grim old sheriff, who had sworn to close any place at once if it were caught giving the workers a less than square deal, had a salutary effect on owners. Ben Ord was known to be as good as his word, and with the tall Ranger to back him up — even though Slade was not known to be a Ranger — there was little doubt that the order would be carried out pronto.

Of course there would be a few shindigs in the course of the celebration. That was to be expected and occasioned little concern. But Slade felt there was no guarantee that Graham wouldn't pull something really serious before the night was over. He reasoned the outlaw chief must be in a furious temper over the debacle of the night before and would be out to even the score in some manner. And, in addition, opportunity for a lucrative haul might well present itself. The town would be bursting with money.

It might also provide a little Ranger opportunity. Slade hoped so; he'd welcome a showdown. Get it over with, one way or another, once and for all. The lethal game of tag he and Neale Graham were playing was becoming a trifle monotonous.

Although the hour was still early, Redmon was already beginning to howl. Later the howl would become a roar. Still later, a raucous screech. At present all was jollity and good fellowship, but when tempers were frayed by alcohol and excitement, it would be otherwise. Differences of opinion would arise, and differences of opinion between such men as these were not settled by courteous parliamentary procedure. Fists would fly, and possibly lead. Payday in a boom town! Broth of the devil's kettle!

Just the same, El Halcon was forced to admit he liked it, liked the excitement and gaiety, with a little seasoning of violence. He chuckled as he recalled reprimanding Marie for just such an attitude.

After making the rounds, Slade and the sheriff repaired to the latter's office to relax with smokes and coffee. The old peace officer was in a cheerful mood despite his pessimistic assertions. Slade knew very well that he was another who took to the hilarity of payday. He wondered, half humorously, half seriously if Ord's prediction of a few nights before had been inspired; if he, too, would still be enjoying such nights when his hair was streaked with silver and there were lines in his face. Could be. Oh, well, "Dead yesterday and unborn tomorrow!"

A couple of the specials dropped in to report that everything appeared to be under control, so far.

Morris Thomas also paid them a visit and accepted a cup of coffee.

"Saw Graham a little while ago," he announced. "He was at the Comstock, drinking with Grimshaw. Seemed to be sort of moody but had recovered from his indisposition. Said he'd be back on the job tomorrow, if he managed to live through payday. Guess that's the way with all of us at our age. All right for youngsters like yourself, Mr. Slade, this heck raising, but when one gets on in years, one craves peace and quiet."

"I've been hearing such sentiments from various quarters of late, but the facts don't seem to bear out the contention," Slade smiled, slanting a meaningful glance at the sheriff, who tried to look innocent and failed signally.

"So the hellion is back in town, eh?" Ord remarked, referring to Neale Graham, after Thomas had departed.

"Thought he would be," Slade said. "Doubtless he would consider it unwise to be absent too long."

"Wonder where he spent the night?" said the sheriff. "Think the bunch might have a hole-up somewhere in the hills?"

"Not beyond the realm of the possible," Slade conceded "That is usual outlaw procedure, a place where they can plan their raids or lie low for a spell if they deem it advisable.

"Of course," he added, "Redmon is different from the average town. They can hang out anywhere here, get together anywhere here without anybody paying them mind. However, I doubt if Graham mingles much with the others here in town; that could be noticed and create comment, which naturally he doesn't desire."

"Guess that's right," Ord agreed. "Well, how about moseyin' over and seeing how the Crow Bait is making out?"

They found the Crow Bait making out very well. Bursting at the seams, in fact. The bar was lined three deep; nearly every table was occupied. The roulette wheels were spinning, the faro bank was doing plenty of business, as were the other games. The girls were already on the floor. The din was deafening, the air thick with smoke. Just tobacco smoke, so far.

Ware had kept their table open and escorted them to it.

"Everything on the house, starting right now and continuing," he said. "Sure got to keep on the good side of the Law tonight; 'pears she's going to be a lulu."

158

"I'd say it's that right now," snorted the sheriff. "Lord, what a racket!"

"The last real payday for the construction workers Redmon will know," Slade said. "By the time another one rolls around, there'll be a camp the other side of the mountains, that will move right along with the steel."

"Oh, the cowhands will manage to keep things fairly lively," replied Ord.

"But I won't be doing the business I am now," observed Ware.

"You'll quite likely be doing more, and a steadier business," Slade said. "I'm going to tell you something, confidentially — I don't want it bruited around. This is going to be a division point, with big yards, a roundhouse, and machine shops. There will be scores of railroaders stationed here, permanently."

"Whe-e-ew!" exclaimed Ware. "That sure makes nice hearing."

"Nice hearing the devil!" wailed the sheriff. "I figured when these hellions moved on we'd have something like peace and quiet."

Neither of his hearers appeared much impressed.

A voice that caused the hanging lamps to quiver announced the presence of Buck Hardy. A few minutes later he came rolling to the table, wanted to buy them a drink, and was quite miffed when he learned Ware had beat him to it.

"Anyhow, Mr. Slade, I guess I can have a dance with your little gal, can't I?" he said.

159

"I can think of no reason why you shouldn't," Slade replied.

Buck ambled back to the bar for another drink before bracing Marie for the dance.

Marie joined them for a few minutes. Her eyes were bright, her cheeks rosy, and she was clothed with gaiety as with a garment.

"This is wonderful!" she exclaimed. "We used to have some nice lively nights in Laredo, didn't we, dear, but nothing like this. I'm having a glorious time. You'll dance with me once tonight, won't you? That will make the evening perfect."

Slade promised to do so and she trotted back to the floor, where Buck was waiting.

Suddenly the sheriff muttered, with an oath,

"Here comes the blankety-blank hellion now!"

"Keep your face straight," Slade cautioned. The sheriff did so, with difficulty.

It was indeed Neale Graham who shouldered his way deftly to the bar and ordered a drink. He did not appear at all perturbed. Quite the contrary, in fact. Which occasioned Slade a qualm of uneasiness. He experienced a premonition which warned that smug look boded no good for somebody. The sheriff's next remark did not help;

"Looks like a cat that's just lapped up a saucer of cream and sees the canary's cage door open. Betcha he's all set to pull something, if he hasn't pulled it already."

"If he has, we'll hear about it," Slade predicted. "However, I think that if he does have something in mind, he'll wait until later, until things are really wild, as they will be before long. Then the risk of attracting attention will be almost nil. He's smart enough to realize that and govern himself accordingly."

"Yes, I expect that will be the way of it," Ord agreed. "And blast it! I feel plumb for certain he will cut loose somehow before this infernal night is over."

Slade did not disagree, for he experienced something of the same feeling and racked his brains in an endeavor to anticipate what the cunning devil might have up his sleeve, with no success.

The night was wearing on and, as Slade predicted, growing wilder by the minute.

The wind was rising, swirling the dust from the streets in clouds that streaked the red, yellow, blue and plaid shirts of the workers but in nowise proved a damper to their enthusiasm. The board sidewalks were packed with a throng of humanity that spilled over into the dust of the streets heedless of the cowhands racing their horses back and forth and whooping to the skies. Song or what was intended for it bellowed over the swinging doors, and a loudening whirl and patter of words. Gold pieces clanged on the "mahogany" echoing the cheerful clink of bottle necks on glass rims. On the dance floors boots thumped and high heels clicked. The musicians strummed and fiddled madly, one with the general spirit of hilarity.

As midnight approached, the scene was unreal, medieval. A dance of Comanches celebrating a victory. A saturnalia of prehistoric cave dwellers under an orbed moon. A revel of ghosts and demons and goblins damned.

Or so it seemed to Walt Slade.

Monstrous, hideous? Perhaps, but nevertheless, colorful and with an undeniable allure. Music and laughter. The days of back-breaking toil forgotten. The days of toil and danger to come unheeded, shrugged away. Might never come, for some of us. No telling whose number is up. So make the most of what we've got, and the devil take the hindmost!

That was the spirit of the throng that jammed Redmon's streets and poured a golden flood into the tills of Redmon's saloons.

And Slade had to admit he was enjoying it as much as the next one, except for the irritating presentiment lurking in the back of his mind that there was real trouble somewhere in the making. Where? Oh, the devil! If it's going to come, it's going to come. Sufficient unto the moment is the evil thereof!

A casuistic philosophy? But maybe, after all, the casuist grasped the true wisdom. He chuckled and ordered another cup of coffee.

162

CHAPTER
EIGHTEEN

"See Hans Ragnal is at the bar with his hands," Ord remarked. "Old as he is — beside him I'm just a younker — he's having the time of his life. Think I'll amble over and palaver with him a bit."

"Not a bad notion," Slade agreed, and settled back comfortably in his chair.

Or tried to. The presentiment of trouble to come was steadily strengthening. Becoming a hunch? Not exactly. A hunch predicated something to do, and at the moment he could think of nothing to do but wait.

A pleasant-faced elderly gentleman strolled in, glancing about with a kindly eye. It was Standish, the paymaster.

Slade caught his attention and gestured to an empty chair. Standish occupied it with a smile and a nod. One of the hustling waiters at once hurried to take the order, shaking his head negatively as Standish reached into his pocket.

"Everybody with Mr. Slade drinks on the house," he chuckled, "boss's order." He skipped to the bar to return with full glasses.

Standish murmured his thanks and gazed at the turbulent activities.

"Well, well, quite a night, thanks to you, Mr. Slade, who made the bust possible. The boys all got paid, I finished my work and decided to take part in the festivities — quite an experience. Closed the coach and made sure the safe was locked good and tight. Still quite a sum of money in that safe."

"How's that?" Slade asked, interested.

"Meat and other provisions for the commissary are paid for in cash," Standish explained. "The cattlemen may not particularly favor, the coming of the railroad, but they are not averse to selling us beef at a nice profit. So we run money in steadily, especially when the paycar rolls, right after which any bills outstanding are paid. Yes, the old box is pretty well loaded. If those devils had succeeded in getting their hands on it they would have made a very nice haul."

"I see," Slade said thoughtfully.

For a while they chatted together, then Standish remarked,

"See Ben Ord is at the bar. If you don't mind, I'll go over for a word or two with him; I've known him for a long time."

"Go right ahead," Slade replied. "He'll be glad to see you."

Standish did so. Slade sat on at the table, his untasted drink before him. Marie was on the floor, dancing with Buck Hardy. Standish and Ord were conversing.

Abruptly, Slade got up, wormed his way through the crowd to the swinging doors and out. Now the

164

presentiment was really a hunch. And explained was Neale Graham's smug expression.

Finally winning free of the celebrants, Slade headed for the railroad yards at a fast pace. When he reached them, he paused and for some moments stood studying the area.

The yards were deserted and very dark, with only the feeble gleams of the switch lights striving to pierce the gloom.

Slade knew the paycar was on a somewhat isolated spur track at the far side of the yards. He hesitated a moment longer, peering and listening, then glided across the network of tracks to the spur.

Nearing the car, he slowed his gait, alert to any sound or movement. There appeared to be neither in the vicinity. It was very dark, with only the one switch light near. But abruptly he was sure that there was a faint glow back of the car windows. He glided forward until he was close to the rear steps. And his sensitive ears caught a sound, a very little sound. Like to the soft whine welling from a sick puppy's throat, but with a metallic rasp no puppy throat could achieve.

And El Halcon understood! Both presentiment and hunch were justified.

He eased a little closer, until he could see the back door of the car; it stood ajar. And through the narrow opening seeped the sound and a dim glow of light.

Slade loosened his guns in their sheaths, waited a moment longer, then, careful to make not the slightest noise, he mounted the steps to the rear platform. Now, in addition to the metallic whine, he heard a low mutter

165

of words. He eased ahead until he could reach the door. His cautious hand touched it and he flung it wide open.

The safe stood near the far end of the coach. The beam of a dark lantern was trained on the door. Before the door squatted a man manipulating a hand drill. Beside him stood two more men, one tall, broad of shoulder, his face in the shadow, who held the dark lantern. Slade's voice blasted at them,

"Up! You're covered!"

All three whirled toward the sound of his voice. The beam of the lantern snapped off and darkness swooped down like a thrown blanket.

Slade drew and shot with both hands, hurling himself to the floor in the same flicker of movement. Answering lead hissed over his prone form. Flat on the floor, he fired again and again, rolling over each time he squeezed the trigger. Slugs fanned his face. He shot at the gun flashes, heard a groaning cry and a thud. Then came a patter of boots on the floor, the crash of the front door flung open. He leaped to his feet, dashed forward, tripped over something on the floor and plunged headlong.

Half stunned by the force of the fall, he floundered a moment in a vain attempt to rise. Another frenzied effort and he regained his feet to hear a beat of hoofs quickly distancing. When he reached the door there was nothing to be seen.

With a muttered oath, he turned back, hopefully struck a match and saw what had tripped him; the body of a man whose life had drained out through his shattered heart and lungs. And instantly El Halcon's hopes were dashed; the dead man was not Neale Graham. Again luck had played into the tricky devil's hands. For Slade was convinced the tall man holding the lantern had been Graham.

The match flickered out. He struck another, spotted the lantern lying on the floor. The slide had been whisked shut, but the lantern was made to burn in any position and had not gone out. He flipped the shade and turned the beam on the safe door. Already several overlapping holes had been drilled around the combination knob. Another twenty minutes and the knob would have been lifted out, the safe opened and rifled of its contents. He had saved the company's money, all right, but again Graham had escaped. As usual, his hair-trigger mind had done exactly the right thing at exactly the right moment.

Still feeling a trifle shaken by the fall, Slade rolled and lighted a cigarette and took a couple of deep drags. He contemplated the corpse and the safe, arrived at a decision. Best to notify the sheriff what had happened without delay. He felt the two outlaws would hardly return, and besides it would take but a few minutes to reach the Crow Bait and come back. He closed the lantern slide before depositing it by the door, and left the car.

Reaching the Crow Bait without undue delay, despite the roaring crowd in the streets, he found Ord and Standish had left the bar for the table. One of the specials and Deputy Boone were with them at the moment.

"Come on with me," Slade told them. "Guess you'd better come along, too, Mr. Standish."

"I knew it! I knew it!" snorted the sheriff. "Let him outa your sight a minute and he's into something. Let's go!"

As they hurried to the yards, Slade tersely acquainted them with what had happened. The sheriff repeated his snort.

Standish exclaimed, "Good heavens! And they tried it again, and again you prevented them from succeeding. How in the world did you catch on to what they were up to?"

"I didn't," Slade replied. "I just figured that if they knew about that money being in the car, which they evidently did, that it would provide them with an excellent opportunity to make a nice haul. So I played my hand that way and it turned out to be a winner, to an extent at least."

"I never heard tell of your equal!" Standish declared. Boone and the special also exclaimed. Ord shot him a keen glance but asked no questions.

When they reached the car, they found everything just as Slade had left it. Standish took one look at the safe and said.

"Ben, suppose we remove the money from that thing and you stow it in your office for the night. Don't reckon anybody will raid that."

"I wouldn't put it past the hellions to try to," growled the sheriff. "Okay, haul it out and we'll pack it along. Boone, round up a couple more of the specials and shuffle that carcass to the office, too. Standish, you might as well amble back to the Crow Bait, tell Ragnal what happened, and wait for us there; we'll be along in a jiffy."

"I'll do that," Standish replied. "Thanks for taking the money; I feel better about it now."

As he and Slade walked to the office, Ord asked, "You figure Graham was one of them?"

"No doubt in my mind as to that," Slade replied. "And again he outsmarted me. His mind works like a well-oiled precision machine. He closed the slide before dropping the lantern, and the sudden transition from light to utter darkness fogged my eyes for an instant and spoiled my aim."

"Didn't outsmart you where that money was concerned," the sheriff said. "Again he missed a nice haul because of you. Just a matter of time till his luck runs out."

"Less of luck and more of outstanding shrewdness and quick thinking, which aren't likely to run out," Slade returned morosely. "Oh, well, as the old saying goes, you can't win 'em all."

They waited at the office until Boone and the specials arrived with the body, which was blanketed on the floor, and then returned to the Crow Bait, where Ragnal and the others were given a more full account of the incident. All were loud in their praise of Slade and exulted in the fact that one of the owlhoots got what was coming to him.

In a last minute decision, Sheriff Ord had the money placed in Ware's Crow Bait safe, which was a new one and would be guarded all night.

"Better there than in my office," Ord said. "Thomas can pick it up tomorrow and take care of his outstanding bills. I'll have a deputy go along with him, just in case. I'm taking no chances with this blankety-blank hell town. I crave a snort!"

A maddening whirl, an immense and incredible hilarity, a wild fling utterly unleashed. But nature was taking toll and Redmon was breathing heavily at last, staggering under its load of excitement and madness, its roar now more the purr of a gorging animal choking over a surfeiting swallow.

Men lurched along the streets, seeking rest. Somewhere a woman screamed, a high-pitched irritated screech, followed by a burst of raucous laughter.

She screeched again, even more angrily. Evidently the recipient thereof did not appreciate somebody's sense of humor. A moment later, however, she joined the laughter. All forgiven!

Redmon's last payday, and its greatest and wildest. But, strange to say, there was no really serious trouble. Some fracases, of course, personal differences of opinion, but nobody was killed, nobody badly injured. No massed conflict that might well have turned out lethal.

The lights were dimming, voices a subdued murmur. The faro dealers were leveling off their chips, the dealers dropping their packs into drawers, the weary drink jugglers pouring nightcaps.

Before the girls left the floor, Slade had the last dance with Marie, as he had promised. He and the sheriff made a final round of the various places and

170

were satisfied everything was under control. They, too, sought rest. And in the sheriff's office the night's single casualty lay stark.

Dawn kindled in the east. The wind had sunk to a whispering breeze that shook down a myriad of dew gems from the grass heads. The sun rose in golden splendor; the rangeland and the mountains were an indescribable beauty. But Redmon did not see it.

Redmon slept!

CHAPTER
NINETEEN

Around noon, Slade, the sheriff, Ragnal, Thomas and Standish enjoyed a late breakfast together, after which they relaxed with drinks and smokes.

"Yep, not a bad night, after all," the sheriff remarked. "One heck of a lot better than I expected."

"And there," remarked Thomas, gesturing toward Slade who had moved to the bar and was conversing with Mack Ware, "and there stands the man responsible. Took just one man of the right sort to bring it about.

"Well, as somebody wrote, nigh two thousand years ago there was a Solitary Life, and it is safe to say that all the armies that ever marched, and all the navies that ever were built, and all the parliaments that ever sat, and all the kings that ever reigned, put together, have not affected the life of man upon this earth as powerfully as has that One Solitary Life!

"In the final analysis, the individual is paramount. One man can influence the destiny of a nation."

The others nodded sober agreement.

Slade himself felt it hadn't been too bad a night, despite the escape of the outlaw chief. He was becoming of the opinion that Graham had but one dependable follower left, which rendered the odds somewhat less lopsided. However, he did not underestimate the tricky and resourceful devil; he was a master of the unexpected, and there was no telling what he might pull without warning. Slade had gone up against formidable opponents in the past but was inclined to think that Neale Graham was in a class by himself and must be recognized as such and dealt with accordingly.

At the office, Doc Clay dropped in with some stragglers and held an impromptu inquest on the body of the slain outlaw. After which Slade rode to the tunnel mouth where he found the work proceeding apace and received hilarious greetings from all sides.

Nearly all the workers were on the job, although he had given orders that nobody's pay should be docked for absence the day after payday.

"Some may not be feeling so good, but they shouldn't have to pay for their night of fun," he explained to Thomas. "That way we'll get the better work from them tomorrow, which will make it up."

After watching the progress of the bore for a while, Slade contacted his three night patrol men.

"Boys," he told them, "there is something I wish you to do for me. At night, somebody keep a watch near the foot of the trail that runs up the slope to the notch. If you see anybody riding that trail during the hours of darkness, let me know about it. Be sure and let me know."

The patrol promised to do so, and Slade knew they would be as good as their word.

"Guess Graham celebrated a mite too much last night, too," Thomas chuckled. "Anyhow, he hasn't showed up so far today. Hope he doesn't suffer a relapse."

Slade failed to mention his opinion that Graham had suffered a decided "relapse" the night before but was likely at the present very much on the mend.

"Sort of playing another hunch, horse," he told Shadow as he rode back to town. "May not mean anything, but if Graham realizes the possibilities of certain conditions as I do, it could mean plenty. A nice chance to really slow up the project. Not impossible that more than one person would die in consequence, but that wouldn't bother him, or deter him. Well, we'll see. Keep your hoofs crossed."

"Uh-huh, and dump you on your blasted ear by so doing," Shadow's answering snort seemed to say.

After stabling his mount, Slade wandered about the town for some time, dropping in at various places, including the Comstock. Redmon was a bit subdued, as was to be expected; this was the aftermath of the payday celebration. For a while he stood watching the glory of the sunset that flooded the mountain crests with polychromatic hues. As dusk was deepening, he again rode to the tunnel mouth, where he found the night shift going strong.

For some time he studied the rate of progress, endeavoring to correlate it with certain figures he had in his head, and arriving at a satisfactory conclusion.

174

One of the patrol approached him. "Nothing so far, Mr. Slade," he reported, "but we're keeping close watch. Nobody is going to ride up that trail without us spottin' 'em."

"I doubt if there will be anybody for a couple of days or so," Slade replied. "But if you do spot somebody, let me know at once. You can almost always find me at the sheriff's office or in the Crow Bait, especially after dark, where I'll be waiting."

That night, while Slade was sitting alone at his table, Neale Graham strolled in, sweeping the room with his pale gaze. He spotted Slade and moved to join him.

"How are you?" the Ranger asked as Graham drew up a chair and motioned to a waiter. "Thomas told me you were slightly indisposed."

"I was, but I'm all right now," Graham replied. "A touch of stomach trouble. Our cooks stir up some very spicy dishes that are perhaps a bit too tasty; one is tempted to over-indulge, arousing a protest from one's innards. I'll be on the job, tomorrow. Didn't get to see much of the payday excitement. Hardly felt up to it."

Marie joined them and Graham asked her to dance. After a couple of numbers he said goodnight.

"Best not to go too strong," he explained. "I want to be on the job tomorrow."

"He didn't have a great deal to say tonight, but appeared to be in a very cheerful mood," the girl told Slade. "Makes me feel he's up to no good."

Slade was inclined to agree. He felt that things were working up to a climax, with a showdown in the offing. Well, the sooner the better.

"Business was slow the early part of the evening, but picking up now," Marie observed. "Shop people and others who were busy last night are having their own little celebration, and there's enough of them to make things lively. Come along and dance with me while we have the chance, which we very likely won't have later. Your hoyden is quite popular, as you may have noticed. Oh, well, as I've said about you, safety in numbers. Let's hoof it, as Buck Hardy would say."

Which was what they were doing when, a little later, Sheriff Ord dropped in and demanded refreshment.

Mack Ware served him and said with a chuckle,

"Guess we'll have to let that 'on the house' custom hold over for another night. After the good work Mr. Slade did last night, I figure it's coming."

When Slade finished a second number with Marie and handed her over to another partner he joined the sheriff.

Ord expressed a view similar to Marie's, that Graham's cheerfulness meant he was up to something.

Slade did not argue the point, for, although he did not mention it, he believed that if his own conclusions were soundly based, he could guess what Graham had in mind. He was not ready to discuss it with anyone, for he had resolved to play a lone hand, trusting he would have a better chance to succeed by himself. He had mapped a definite plan of action and was determined to follow it. If any of the angles turned out to be erroneous, especially the assumption that Graham had but one follower left, he would very likely pay the ultimate price for so doing, but that he would risk.

Doctor Sam Clay, the coroner, put in an appearance, looking jovial and expectant.

"What, no business tonight?" he asked in disappointed tones. "Oh, well, the night's young."

"You're a regular old ghoul!" Ord declared. "Battening on carcasses."

Doc winked at Slade and ordered drinks.

"Hear anything from old man Dunn?" the sheriff asked of Slade.

"Not a word," the Ranger replied. "Hardly expected to, though. Very likely he'll come booming in any day now, without previous announcement. He does things like that."

"Guess he figures there's no need to bother his head about over here, knowing everything will be taken care of," Ord said.

"He could be disappointed," Slade smiled.

"Uh-huh, and the moon could be made of green cheese, but I doubt it," the sheriff retorted.

"Your gal looks plumb chipper," he added, with an appreciative glance toward the dance floor. "Figure she really enjoyed the hell raising last night."

"Like some other folks I could mention, who won't admit it," Slade said.

The old sheriff snorted, refused to concede the implication and ordered a drink.

Several peaceful days followed, as peaceful as days ever were in Redmon. Slade spent much time in the tunnel, checking the progress made, conferring with Thomas and Flaherty.

And as the tunnel bored steadily through the irritating shale, the shoring following close behind the drillers and the shovels, he began to grow uneasy. Began to look like his hunch might not be a straight one.

Graham had returned to work and showed no signs of perturbation; was cheerful and complacent. Which didn't help. Seemed that if he really intended to make the move Slade expected, he should have done it already.

And then, the fourth night, one of the cutting patrolmen hurried into the Crow Bait, where Slade was sitting alone at his table.

"Two fellers rode up the trail a little better than an hour ago, Mr. Slade," he announced. "I got here quick as I could. Figured you didn't want it to look too obvious what I was up to and hung around until there was nobody nearby and then hightailed."

"Good man!" Slade applauded. "You did just right, and you've been a big help. Over to the bar and have some drinks before you go back to the cut."

The patrolman, grinning broadly, did as he was told. Slade gestured to Ware, who nodded his understanding.

Waving to Marie on the floor, who looked decidedly worried, Slade left the Crow Bait and headed for Shadow's stable at a fast pace. He cinched up quickly, led the horse out and mounted.

"Well, here we go, horse," he said. "It's showdown, no doubt in my mind as to that — my hunch was a straight one. So rattle your hocks, cayuse, we've sure got things to do. Only hope I'm not too late. An hour would provide plenty of time for the devils to set their trap. Absolutely necessary that we get there before they spring it. Let's go!"

Shadow responded, stretching his long legs, slugging his head above the bit and snorting gaily, for he loved these night ambles. Slade did not curb him until they neared the cutting. Peering ahead through the gloom of an overcast sky, he could see nobody near. He bypassed the cut and rode up the winding trail. Reaching the notch, he slowed the horse's gait, for here it was almost black dark and there was no telling what he might meet in the misty murk.

However, he made it to the far slope without incident, pulled to a halt, and for a moment gazed down toward the prairie, which was a little silvered by the veiled starshine. He put Shadow to the sag and descended to the level ground. Glancing about he spotted the dim forms of two horses tethered to branches. Evidently the outlaws were in the cave, at work. He sent Shadow past the two cayuses and a little farther, leaving him where he was practically invisible against the growth. At a dead run he headed for the cave mouth.

It was really black dark, but Slade did not hesitate. He sped into the bore with quick light steps that made hardly any sound. Without slackening his pace he followed the curve, hugging the cave wall. He was almost to where the curve levelled off to the straight-away when he heard voices. He slowed a little, hands close to the butts of his guns.

Light showed around the curve. Another moment and he saw its source. It came from a flare carried by a squat, brawny man who bulged into view. Beside him was Neale Graham. They were moving swiftly, laughing and talking exultantly, evidently sure they had accomplished their purpose. Slade's voice rang through the cave, for he knew there was not an instant to lose;

"Elevate! In the name of the State of Texas! Under the authority of the Texas Rangers!"

There were startled exclamations as they saw his tall form outlined in the glow of the flare. Neale Graham yelled, a high-pitched screech of maniacal fury, and went for his guns, as did the other.

Weaving, dodging, Slade drew and shot as lead whined past him. A slug struck the cave wall, showered his face with stinging fragments and ricocheted off into space. Half blinded, he squeezed both triggers.

The squat man fell on his face, to lie motionless. The guttering flare dropped from his lifeless hand but did not go out. Graham lined sights.

Then abruptly he went rigid, raising himself on his tip-toes. For an instant he stood erect, his guns clattering on the rock floor. He reeled sideways and into the river. The black water closed over him with a sullen splash.

CHAPTER
TWENTY

Slade did not wait to see if he was dead or drowning, but raced up the bore. Another moment and he saw what he expected to see; a sputter of sparks flowing steadily toward the side of the cave. With a mighty effort, he increased his speed, reached that crawl of sparks that was death's reaching hand, dropped to his knees beside it. The faint glow showed one of the big crevices packed with dynamite, and the burning fuse was scant inches from the detonating cap. There was not a second to lose.

The crevice was filled almost to the brim with the dynamite sticks, and because of a slight overhang of the stone he could barely reach the fuse. He gripped it between his thumb and finger; put forth all of his great strength, squeezing the fuse together. Whipping out his clasp knife, he opened it with his teeth and strained forward. He could just touch the fuse with an inch or so of the blade and could put very little pressure on the knife.

The sparks rained onto his hand, searing his flesh. He grimly endured the torment, for he knew if he flinched, the fire would get past his clamping fingers, flow over the cap and set off the explosion that would blow him into eternity, crash down the cave wall and pour the river into the railroad tunnel, flooding it from end to end and very likely drowning half the night shift working there.

Frantically he sawed at the tough fibre of the fuse, which resisted stubbornly. Pain was flowing through his hand, unheeded. He put forth a last frenzied effort, felt the fuse part under the sawing pressure of the knife edge. He flung the smoking thing into the river and sank against the cave wall, shaking as with ague, his muscles turned to water, utterly spent.

For long minutes he lay as motionless as the dead outlaw beyond the bend. The aftermath of intense relief after the terrible seconds of apprehension almost paralyzed him. Finally he got to his feet, unsteadily, leaned against the rock wall and rolled and lighted a cigarette with fingers that still trembled a little. Several deep drags of the fragrant smoke soothed his tortured nerves. His left hand, the one that had clamped the fuse, smarted, but he paid it little mind. Pinching out the butt, he struck another match and examined the cache of explosive in the crevice. There were enough sticks to blow the mountain down. As usual, Graham had been thorough.

Making his way around the bulge of the curve, he saw the flare was still burning, outlining the stark form of the dead outlaw, Graham's fallen guns lying beside him. With hardly a glance at the fellow, he continued to the mouth of the cave, instinctively slowing and studying the area before stepping from the bore, although he was convinced that there was nothing more to fear from Neale Graham, that he was either dead from the slug that had ripped through his chest, or had drowned in the black water.

Pausing to strip the rigs from the outlaw horses and turn them loose, he made his way to where Shadow waited and swung into the saddle, marvelling at the effort required. Undoubtedly he had been very close to utter and dangerous exhaustion. Once again he glanced around before riding out from the shadow.

"The hellion has pulled so many unexpected capers, I guess I'm half wondering if he can manage to finagle an untimely resurrection," he told the horse. "Guess not. Let's go."

Slade didn't pause at the cutting but rode on. Half way to town he met the patrolman trudging back to work.

"Everything okay?" he called as he sighted the Ranger.

Slade reined in and told him, in detail, exactly what had happened. The patrolman clucked admiration in his throat.

"And Graham was the real head scoundrel!" he exclaimed in astonishment. "Just goes to show you never can tell where the lightning will strike. Just wait till I tell the boys. Again you saved some of 'em from getting their comeuppance. We won't forget, Mr. Slade, we won't forget."

Very likely he anticipated that resounding roar,

"Hurrah for the Old Man!"

At the edge of town, Slade reined in and for a moment sat gazing back toward the gleaming ribbons of steel that now, unhindered by ruthless schemers, would flow on to complete their conquest of the Thunder Trail.

When he reached the Crow Bait, after stabling Shadow and giving him a good rubdown, Slade found Marie and the sheriff anxiously waiting. He repeated the story of the encounter in the cavern, leaving his hearers convinced they had not heard and never would a full account of the grim happenings.

"Graham was a competent and highly trained engineer and geologist," he concluded. "He plotted the course of the tunnel in relation to the underground river and realized that the wall between the cave and the tunnel was, comparatively speaking, not overly thick. Plenty strong to resist any ordinary impact, even that of a derailed engine, but not strong enough to resist a hundred sticks of dynamite, which is just about the amount in that crevice. A very shrewd and carefully contrived scheme that came close to working."

"But you figured it all out, too," commented the sheriff.

"I realized the possibilities, and played a hunch that Graham did also and would try to put just such a plan into effect, which he did," Slade replied.

"Yep, he was smart, but not quite smart enough to go up against El Halcon," Ord said.

Just about his normal self again, Slade ordered something to eat and submitted to Marie's ministering to his scorched hand; the burns were really only superficial.

184

"And you figure Graham is dead, all right," Ord remarked.

"Yes, I think so," Slade replied. "I'm convinced my bullet got him right over the heart, and he went into the river, which is deep and would have carried off his body. Guess we'll never know for sure, but I reckon we can presume him dead."

"Yep, he's a goner," said the sheriff. "Good riddance; the world's better off without him. I'll fetch in that body tomorrow, and the horses, if they're still around. Yep, finished business. Now maybe we'll have something like peace around here for a change."

"I'll go along with you, and make sure that charge of dynamite is lifted out properly, against the chance of it going off by accident and blowing the mountain down," Slade said. "Well, I'm in favor of calling it a night as soon as I've finished eating. Been quite a night, everything considered. I'll see Thomas tomorrow."

"I'm going to change," Marie said and skipped off to the dressing room.

Morris Thomas was amazed and saddened at learning of Graham's duplicity and his tragic end.

"Strange I never caught on," he remarked. "He had me fooled completely; I thought him a fine person."

"You are an engineer, not a law enforcement officer," Slade pointed out. "The training for the two professions is somewhat different."

"And you are both," Thomas said.

Slade smiled, and did not contradict.

The following day, not particularly to Slade's surprise, Jaggers Dunn's private car rolled in. He and Slade had a long talk, with everything explained in detail.

"Chalk up another one for you," Dunn said when the tale was finished. "Now everything should go smoothly. And maybe the M. K. hellions will lay off again for a while."

"Yes, I think they will," Slade agreed. "They won't know for sure how much we may have learned of Graham's connections with them, before he died. Which should deter them from any activity for the present, at least."

At the Crow Bait, later, Slade told Marie and the sheriff.

"I promised Dunn I'd stick around until the tunnel is driven through, just to make certain everything is as it should be. Once that is done he should encounter no real difficulties."

"And then," Marie said softly, "the trail that winds over the hill!"